CW01658950

Sir, There's a Pig in t'Yard

by

John Riley

First published in Great Britain by Pen Press

All paper used in the printing of this book has been made from wood grown in managed, sustainable forests.

ISBN13: 978-1-78003-012-8

Printed and bound in the UK
Pen Press is an imprint of Indepenpress Publishing Limited
25 Eastern Place
Brighton
BN2 1GJ

A catalogue record of this book is available from the British Library

Cover design by Jacqueline Abromeit

Acknowledgements

I would like to thank all my family for their unfailing support throughout the writing and ultimate publishing of this diary.

Special thanks to my wife Pam whose enthusiasm and encouragement ensured its completion.

Thanks also for the unwitting contribution of staff and pupils of "Lees Bank Special School" of whom I have fond and happy memories.

Finally, gratitude to Claire of "Penpress" for her efficiency, thoughtfulness and energy throughout.

All the events in this book are based on the author's true experiences. Names have been changed for privacy reasons, however.

'Timothy Winters'

Timothy Winters comes to school
With eyes as wide as a football-pool,
Ears like bombs and teeth like splinters:
A blitz of a boy is Timothy Winters.

His belly is white, his neck is dark,
And his hair is an exclamation-mark.
His clothes are enough to scare a crow
And through his britches the blue winds blow.

When teacher talks he won't hear a word
And he shoots down dead the arithmetic-bird,
He licks the pattern off his plate
And he's not even heard of the Welfare State.

Timothy Winters has bloody feet
And he lives in a house on Suez Street,
He sleeps in a sack on the kitchen floor
And they say there aren't boys like him anymore.

Old Man Winters likes his beer
And his missus ran off with a bombardier,
Grandma sits in the grate with a gin
And Timothy's dosed with an aspirin.

The Welfare Worker lies awake
But the law's as tricky as a ten-foot snake,
So Timothy Winters drinks his cup
And slowly goes on growing up.

At Morning Prayers the Master helves
For children less fortunate than ourselves,
And the loudest response in the room is when
Timothy Winters roars 'Amen!'

So come one angel, come on ten
Timothy Winters says 'Amen
Amen amen amen amen.'
Timothy Winters, Lord. Amen

Charles Causley

MONDAY

11th November

8:45 am. Back into the house for the third time! This time it's the burglar alarm. It's on all right, but it's just that I can't remember actually *doing* it. Already I've had to go back for my briefcase then for my flask. If there's anything else it'll have to stay at home.

Wish I could! What a lousy day. Just beginning to really pour down and I get soaked dashing between the house and the car. Serves me right. I just wish I could remember things first time. Surely senility shouldn't be setting in before forty, even though it is only a week away.

At last we're off. A twenty-minute journey, half of it made up of heavy traffic, cursing, trying to overtake in stupid places just because I won't set off five minutes earlier; the other half a tranquil meander through leafy country lanes along the 'scenic route'. I found it quite by chance one day when traffic had come to a complete halt due to an accident up ahead and I've stuck to it ever since. It's a bit further and takes a bit longer but when the weather's right, it's bliss!

Trouble is that lately I've found myself looking enviously at the postman, the milkman, the council gardener. Last week's weather was autumn perfection and these guys seem to go about their jobs at their own pace – stop for a chat if you like – do a bit more – no pressure. That's it – NO PRESSURE! That's the trouble with our job just now. It's *all* pressure! We seem to be getting more than our share of other people's troubles. They have kids who give them nightmares – don't want to learn, always in bother, so what do they do? Of course! Get them referred to a Special School. I mean, that's what they're for after all. It's really doing the kid a favour. He doesn't fit in here for all we've tried. There, he'll get individual attention, his work will perk up, he'll take an interest in school again and I shall live happily ever after!

What *actually* happens is that generally it's too late to recapture any spark of interest in schooling, and often they have only a year or so before they're due to leave so they while away the fruitless hours by cultivating our own troublemakers, actual and latent, who only need a lead to develop their potential to the full. The net result is that what, until recently, has been an easy-going, contented, *caring* place, has suddenly been stood on its head. Lord! What thoughts and already it's only Monday morning. One good thing though – I just passed a postman and he doesn't look too thrilled with life today, with rain dripping off his nose-end.

Another five minutes and the spell is broken. *Au revoir* leafy lanes, albeit sodden ones today, sharp left past the signs 'Lees Bank Special School'. Hell fire! I shall have to send one volunteer or pressed man (same thing) down the drive with a bucket of hot water, soap and a brush to scrub the appendix 'For Nutters', (in brackets), which has been scrawled yet again under the school name on the boards. I'll mangle whoever it is if I'm ever lucky enough to catch them at it!

9:00 am. On up the drive and find somewhere to park in the space reserved for staff cars. God! Don't some of this lot go home even for the weekend? I've actually tried (only once or twice mind) arriving an hour early and *still* I could barely find room to squeeze in. This morning is no exception but just as I'm about to give up and park at the neck of the drive, risking the wrath of the coach drivers, I find a little gap and manage to wriggle into it. Getting the car *in* is one thing, getting myself *out* is another thing entirely.

After doing a Houdini, complete with briefcase and umbrella (not to be recommended for those not in the peak of condition), I manage to find enough space with much puffing and cursing, to stand upright and turn round, only to come face to face with the 'Ambassador of This Week's Problems', Walter Willis. Walter is not his real name, he got it through an application for a job that he once wrote out, which apparently required a 'Walter'. Actually it all turned out that the advert was for a *waiter* in a posh hotel in town. However, the name stuck and appeals to him so much that he now refuses to answer to his real name – Keith. It's quite a shock I can tell you first thing on a Monday morning to turn round and find yourself apparently looking down the wrong end of a pair of binoculars. Walter's specs are so thick that that's the effect you get. His enthusiasm and his anxiety to please are really quite moving especially this early – unfortunately it's not meant to last.

"Um – um, morning, Sir."

Wearily but with a genuine effort, "Morning, Walter. You're here bright and early. Thought the rain might have kept you at home with your catarrh."

"Oh, no – um – Sir – um – I don't like not to come to school, Sir."

Course he doesn't, poor lad! With his home life I think I would have felt the same way.

"Um – Sir – um – John Bott has just been in the girls' toilets AGAIN!"

"Oh, jeeze! Walter, you meet me every morning of the week and always it's a complaint or a tale about something or a tale about somebody. Look – tell Bott that if he's that keen to spend his time in the girls' toilets, I'll set him on cleaning them out. Open the car boot – right? See the pile of newspapers – right? Pick them up and take them down the cellar and put them with the rest – OK?" We collect newspapers and sell them to help the school fund.

"Um – Sir – um no, I don't like going down the cellar. Um – it's dark and um – I can't see and-um-last time I tore my coat."

"Well then, take John Bott with you. It'll keep him out of bother."

Look of panic on Walter's face. "Um – no – um – Sir. When I go down the cellar with him-um-um-he puts his hand down my trousers and does that." The following mime needs no explanation.

"Oh boy! He's worse than I thought. Listen, Walter – are you listening? Watch my lips—just go and find somewhere quiet, right out of the way and see how long you can stay there without getting into bother."

"Yessir," though the idea doesn't really seem to appeal.

Walter is the complete masochist you see. He likes to be in the thick of the action all the time. I'm always into John Bott's ribs for some misconduct or other, usually due to Walter grassing. Bott, in turn, knows the source of my information and gives Walter a leathering because Walter is a human punchbag, no resistance, and Bott is the complete sadist. I always used to put a stop to it, but it was like trying to reverse the laws of the jungle. Luckily for Walter, physical pain doesn't seem to bother him – not that he's a tough lad, quite the reverse in fact. It's just that it doesn't trouble him. He feels it, but in a strange way he seems to get a kick out of it. Sorry!

That's enough of Walter for starters so turning my back on him, out of sight out of mind. I pay my ritual morning visit to the office – no mail – on to the staff room; pick up my registers, mutter, "Morning". Half reply, the other half ignore. None of them look any more cheerful than I feel. Can't understand why they come an hour early if they are going to fret and fidget their way to the starting line. Might as well have instant depression than the kind that creeps up slowly over an hour. We've talked about this often in the staff room. It's not laziness or lack of commitment on my part (that's my story anyway). I just prefer to get there, take a couple of deep breaths and get stuck in, whereas others would rather relax and acclimatise gradually. A bit like the difference between diving straight into the sea and testing it with your big toe first.

My longish drive to school gives me an advantage. I can compose myself, listen to the car radio and generally wind down, whereas most of the others live on the doorstep.

9:15 am. Fifteen minutes to lift-off! I walk across the yard from the 'Barracks', which houses the admin section and lower school, to my patch, the 'Mansion'. This is a lovely old mansion, the original home of a wealthy local family. It is now shared by the Leavers' Group and The Units – little tots who are there to be assessed, processed and then put in the right pigeonhole when they start to develop. The Leavers' room and my office are the top floor, the tots occupy the ground floor and we all exist amicably together.

Right at the top of the building in a cosy flat under the roof lives Little Albert, our long-suffering caretaker, his wife Edna, and Savage Beast. Mr and Mrs Light, to give them their correct title, are a pleasant, accommodating couple. Savage Beast is distinctly less pleasant but, I must agree, a necessity in a place so remote and such a prey to vandalism and other sorts of nightly terror. Its real name is Laddy or Rover or something equally inspired. I never get near enough to actually address it by name. I reckon I can get on with most animals, but this fearsome canine version of a werewolf (the Incredible Hulk) scares the pants off me.

At 1:00 pm precisely each day, the corridors and doorways of the 'Mansion' empty magically, for that's the time that Savage Beast has his walkies (sing the last phrase to the tune of *Teddy Bear's Picnic* if you like). Doors are closed and all that can be heard is a scrattering of claws on the floorboards, followed by a strangulated gargling, followed by heavier footfalls as Albert strives to get a grip and keep his balance. The fire escape doors open and then bang shut, and once in the fresh air, Savage Beast heads for the woods with Albert rattling along behind like an old tin can tied to a wedding car bumper.

Anyway, I digress. It's still only 9:16 am and by this time I've climbed the stairs and had a quick look into the Leavers' room.

Thank goodness nobody has seen me peek round the corner. Most of them are in there already, all talking at once about the weekend, no one listening to a word.

"Four pints down at t'Mason's Arms on Sat'day neet. Wi me dad wa'n't ah?"

"Adam Ant? He's CRAP!"

"Shoulda seen t'Town. Bet Bury 3–0 yah! Look at Towers. He ran on t'pitch when we scored and t'coppers kicked him in!"

"It's a beauty. Ten gears an I went to York on it on Sunday."

Leave them to it for a while. Let them settle down and run out of steam. There's more important business first. The buses. All our kids, with the exception of the Leavers, are 'bussed' to school. These arrive in convoy up the drive, disgorge their contents as if a gigantic plug has been pulled out of a bath, then take themselves off again, leaving the kids to rush, trumpeting like wounded elephants, into the playground.

My office window looks directly over the square where the buses stop. I don't know why, after nearly twenty years in the game, but I always feel nervous those few minutes before the buses arrive each morning. I stand there, tensed, feeling like General Custer waiting for Sitting Bull's charge. I wait and watch each bus empty, looking for signs of trouble. It can start in a flash and the buses parked side by side make ideal ambush spots for scores, started but stifled on the way to school, to be settled, or for the timid to be terrified by the bullies who jump out on them and mug them without being seen.

Many's the time I've caught up with the offenders a little later in the day and filled them in on the exact details of their particular little skirmish. The difficulty is to keep a straight face as their eyes and mouths open wider and wider as they realise that they have been well and truly rumbled. The question is invariably, "How did you know, Sir?" The answer is equally invariable, "Don't forget lad, I *always* know and see *everything*!" A colossal piece of conceit and bluff, but it works like a charm with the younger ones, a bit like Santa Claus. The older ones are more sceptical, but amazingly, nobody has yet fathomed the secret. They know it's a con, but they can't see anything up my sleeve.

9:20 am. Happily the rain has stopped though it doesn't seem totally convinced that it ought to have done and looks ready to go back into action again any second. Still, it means that they can all have five minutes of fresh air to work off a bit of energy before being cooped up inside for the next hour or so. I take a couple of deep breaths before going down below – a bit like a Polynesian pearl diver.

Incredibly for a Monday, there has not been a single incident getting off the buses. It can't last! I am just in time to be greeted by the stragglers. These are inevitably the physically handicapped youngsters whose crutches or leg irons hold them back, but who are always the ones with the big smiles and ready welcomes. We shuffle and clomp together up to the yard to where Eileen Black, one of the Non-Teaching Assistants (NTAs) is looking distinctly harassed. There should be an NTA and a teacher on duty in the yard at all times, to quote the book, but not this time as it happens, and it is Monday morning. It's quite touching to see the look of enormous relief as she sees the US Cavalry approaching.

"I am so glad to see you – morning – sorry!" getting more flustered than ever. "Will you just go round the corner by the dustbins for a minute? I'm sure there's something going on round there."

Oh great, 'Smokers' Corner' is what we call the area by the dustbins. Shielded by a protecting wall, it's the ideal spot for the job. The smokers can carry on, sheltered both from the cold wind and from unwanted observers. An additional advantage is that a lookout posted on the corner wall can casually monitor all enemy activity. On this occasion I see Charles Delaney on sentry-duty, which is no bad thing because at least I don't have to go through the trauma of interrogation, abuse, discovery, abuse, punishment, abuse, with him.

He is at the moment, as far as authority is concerned, public enemy number two. Anyone less like a 'Charles' would be hard to imagine. Violent, foul-mouthed, unreasonable, he really can make life a misery when he's in that mood. As I close nonchalantly, under cover of idle chatter to some marbles players, Charles casually inclines his head and mutters something out of the far corner of his mouth. I cover the last few yards in a couple of bionic leaps, which bring me face to face with the company of sinners (three black, two white and one khaki, as they say). In addition to Charles, there is the exotically-named Delroy de Lancey (public enemy number one, and black), Freddie Morrison (black), Arthur Davis (alias 'The Pink Panther', black), Peter Howard (white) and Javed Mohinder (khaki). The startled looks, the sudden clenching of a fist and the simultaneous rolling of the fingers by big Freddie Morrison tell it all.

I reach out, palm upwards, "All right – let's have it".

"Have what? I don't know what you mean—Sir."

"The tab you just screwed up in your fist."

The others look on expressionlessly, taking no part. It isn't time for force yet though. He hesitates.

"Come ON," sharply now.

Reluctantly the hand stretches out, fingers underneath and drops into my hand—a torn-up bus ticket! In a flash they're all jumping around clapping their thighs, falsetto West Indian laughs, fingers pointing at me. "We seen you comin' roun' the corner –

we seen y'all the way. We knew what you was after. We *fooled* you man."

Off they go again, hooting and slapping their hands together. I give Freddie a playful cuff on the ear. "Comic! Don't worry though – I've had you before and I'll have you again. Sooner than you think probably."

I really am pleased though. Obviously they weren't smoking – probably skint after the weekend anyway. Besides, the joke, especially with these hardcases, gets things off to a good-natured start, which is a great bonus on a miserable Monday morning, when the emotional temperature can be set for a week. There's still a point to be made though.

"OK lads I fell for it *but* just let me remind you, Smokers' Corner is out of bounds to everybody, so spread yourselves around the yard where you can be seen *all* the time by whoever is on duty, without having to be looked for. Arthur and Peter, you two know better. I've asked you a dozen times to stay out of the yard. I expect an example from the Leavers."

They slope off, grinning furtively to each other, the long and the short of it. Arthur, six feet, immensely powerful and very deep, his stooping profile as he turns the corner out of the yard a clue to the nickname 'The Pink Panther'. Peter, short, stocky, belligerent but shallow in contrast to his inseparable companion.

9:30 am. Everybody in and I go back upstairs. All there apart from Andrew Miller, which is no surprise, Shirley Baker and Carol Crawford. Quick ticks against all the other names.

"Where's Miller – on nights again this week?" Giggles and guffaws greet this devastating piece of wit.

"Anybody seen Shirley and Carol?"

"THEY'RE AT PLAY-SCHOOL. THEY GO EVERY MONDAY AND YOU ALWAYS FORGET," Luke Towers, a skinny youth with a thunderous voice which makes everything sound like an accusation, reminds me.

"You'll have to speak up, it's hard to hear what you're saying when you mutter like that," I say with what I regard as blistering irony.

"I said—"

"Oh! Forget it – I just remembered where they are. Dinner

money please. I hope you've all remembered to bring the exact amount this week." Whoever thought of eighty-seven pence was a logical figure wants condemning to a life sentence of solitary confinement spent working out the change from a one pound note, ten million times! The extra thirteen pence to round it up wouldn't break anyone.

The first four come out, predictably slap a sheet each on the table and stand there woodenly, waiting for their change.

"I don't know what the hell you're standing there like stuffed owls for. I HAVEN'T GOT ANY CHANGE. THAT'S WHY I ASK YOU TO BRING THE CORRECT AMOUNT!" Simmer down, simmer down! There, I've failed the first real test of the week. Lost my cool at the first jump. That won't do at all. Proceed with dignity for the rest of the operation.

Happily, out of the remaining ten, seven have brought the right amount so that helps. Totting the hatefully odd amounts and making them balance at the end is the worst thing though and I am being distracted by a small person standing silently by my table. Out of the corner of my eye I recognise her as Little Girl in Party Dress. She's from lower down the school, a pale, timid little creature who always wears this party dress thing, winter and summer alike. It's almost white so presumably it must get washed from time to time. I have to ignore her for the moment as the calculations have reached the critical stage and the whole school meals system could stand or fall by what happens in the next few seconds.

"Sir." Silence.

"Sirrr—" Silence plus angry frown.

"SIR!"

Dam bursts. "WHAT?" accompanied by a clatter as Little Girl jumps out of her skin and scatters carefully assembled piles of coins all over the table and floor. Chaos ensues as everyone dives in to help. Little Girl howls, heartbroken, and I have fallen at the second fence too.

"Sorry, pet," I try ingratiatingly to console her. "But I was trying to add all that money up and I'm not very good at it you see. Now, what do you want?"

She copes with the tears by lifting up the bottom of the dress revealing knickers a few shades less white than the dress even, and mopping her eyes with it. After a further period of reproach for me by way of sniffing and hiccuping, she composes herself sufficiently to whisper, "Mr Cookland wants to know if you've got the Munchkins?"

"No, love. Tell him I always walk like this."

She obviously has no more idea of what I'm talking about than I have of what she is (if you see what I mean). My lot fall about cackling wickedly as they always do whenever we play at 'Bait The Messenger'. However, on this occasion I must admit I am at a complete loss. Standards must be kept up though, and no messenger, however timid or sensitive, may be allowed to leave with sanity intact.

"No, Sir. Mr Cookland wants to know if he can have the Munchkins?"

"Er – yes he can, but warn him that it can be very serious at his age."

Little Girl by now is obviously firmly convinced that there is only one sane person in the room and is nervously looking round for possible means of escape, when Luke (Mouth of the Year) Towers comes to the rescue with an explanation in a voice which must have registered on the Richter Scale.

"HE WANTS 'EM FOR T'CHRISTMAS PLAY YOU DAFT THING."

"Hey – less of the 'daft thing' or you'll be waking up with a crowd round your bed. What is the Christmas play anyway this year?"

"IT'S *T'WIZARD OF OZ* AND—"

"Will you shut up for a bit and let somebody else have a chance to speak. You're beginning to make the windows rattle." Looking round for a soothing voice I see Louise Hey, a quiet, sweet-natured girl.

"Louise, would you please explain just what this little person is after."

"YOU DON'T TALK TO ME ALL NICE LIKE YOU TALK TO HER."

"I wouldn't talk to you at all if I wasn't paid to."

"HUH. CHARMING!"

"Louise, carry on please, love."

"LITTLE CREEP!"

"This is the last time I'll warn you, fat mouth. Now button it."

"Well, Sir – the Munchkins are the little people in *The Wizard of Oz* but I don't think there are any in our class. I think they're all from lower down the school."

"Thank you, Louise. All right, petal? Tell Mr Cookland that we don't want any today and thank him for the interruption. We all enjoyed it so much. It was just what we needed first thing on a Monday morning."

Little Girl nods and wastes no time in making her escape from the madhouse.

9:35 am. Ten minutes before going across to assembly where I can regroup my personal forces for a quarter of an hour or so at the back of the hall-cum-dining room. Another knock at the door.

"Come in." Enter 'Kermit' real name Jeremy Crawley. Under his nose already is his customary green moustache, an effect produced by constantly wiping his cuff across his ever-dripping nose. Kermit is another punch-bag. Any kind of attention is better than none, is his motto. So whether it's being kicked round the yard by a dozen other kids, flushed head first down the lavatory or very occasionally rewarded with a word of encouragement, it all comes alike to him.

"Well – what is it now?" I suppose I could be a bit more welcoming, but visitors are low on my list of favourite people right now. However, Kermit is not the least bit discouraged. His facial expression, in sickness or in health, is always one of pure joy. He beams radiantly as he tilts his head back in order to see through one of the minute portions of his thick specs as yet not cracked, scuffed, or otherwise gunged-up. More often than not though, he has either lost or 'mislaid' them and half the day is wasted in retracing his movements from leaving home to either finding them or leaving it till tomorrow.

"Greetings, Kermit – we're over here," I try again as he still hesitates, triffid-like, waving his head trying to locate the voice exactly. Satisfied eventually that he is on course, he launches himself across the room in the direction of my desk, only to go crashing to the floor over John Bott's foot, strategically-placed in the aisle by the first desk.

"Nice one, Kermit. Only six more hurdles and you win the

gold medal. Now I suppose there must be a message or did you really come in to practise for the Olympics?"

Unperturbed, he picks himself up, and accompanied by a chorus of hoots and jeers, safely negotiates the few remaining steps between us. Nodding his head with each word as if to emphasise its accuracy, he proudly announces, "Mrs Dolan says you haven't forgot to put the chairs out in the hall 'cos it's your day."

"Champion! I knew it would snow as soon as I saw you walk through that door. Tell Mrs Dolan OK I had forgotten but OK we'll do it."

Kermit leaves us, hunched-up, head bobbing as he mentally recites the message to himself on the way back across the landing. At the other side of the landing lives the other half of the Leavers' Group. We split them in two because of the large numbers. Mary Dolan, a tiny but very competent woman, is in charge of the other half.

"Right, lovely boys! Away you go – come on now – move yourselves move yourselves!" This last bit is my proud imitation of Sergeant-Major Windsor Davies. It helps to hurry them along as they drag themselves unwillingly across to the hall to see to the chairs. It's a pity about the imitation though. I think it's great but none of them ever watch BBC. I think they could all get degrees in *Emmerdale* or *Coronation Street* but when it comes to real class stuff—

9:40 am. Just as I am reading the riot act to the girls about coming across to assembly on time mind you, and not everybody else is on their way back and a few other things besides while I'm at it, there comes yet another knock at the door.

"Stuff me gently!" It was meant to be an aside but draws "Oohs!" and other assorted shocked reactions from the girls who hear everything but what they're supposed to.

"COME IN." He comes in – a boy from the middle school.

"YES!" He wilts.

"WELL!" He dithers and starts gabbling.

"Misswoodsezterdoprayerscosshezgorrervisitor."

"Do you speak English too?"

"Eh?"

“Pardon?”

“Pardon.”

“It just sounded like a foreign language. All I could make out was Miss Wood and a visitor. Now do I understand that Miss Wood wants me to take assembly because she has a visitor? Is that it?”

“Yes, Sir.”

“Well, why didn’t you say so?”

“Sorry, Sir.”

“I should think so. On your bike and tell Miss Wood I’ll be over in a couple of minutes. Oh, by the way, ask her how she knew it was my birthday today. She’ll understand.”

She’ll understand all right! Next to the electric chair, Monday morning assembly is the experience I can most do without.

Away shoots the messenger with me close behind. It doesn’t do to leave my lads organising the chairs for too long by themselves or the result is likely to be chaos. They either get them too near the front or get the rows so close together that people can’t sit down properly or more likely still, they all stand around waiting for someone else to make a start. Luckily this time, they have at least begun the operation and haven’t got far enough to make a pig’s ear of it so I join in the fun, putting out just one chair as a marker for the end of each row and then they fill in the rest of the row.

As a result of all the delays to date, we only just finish the job before the first of the faithful arrive to pray. Fortunately, Monday morning assembly only involves the senior and middle schools so only the minimum seating arrangement is necessary.

Charles Delaney goads the record player into providing some ‘incidental light music’ to soothe the mind and set the right mood for the show, but sets it at a level that would shatter a row of beer glasses. In his embarrassment and confusion he grabs at the volume control but only succeeds in catching the stylus, a blow that sends it screeching across the face of the disc. Joe Johnson, his class teacher, whose pride and joy the record is, dives in and retrieves the situation, simultaneously giving Charles his umpteenth ‘last warning’ should anything like it happen again. Normally, Charles would hit the roof at being shown-up in this way, but being in charge of the record player at assembly is such a prestigious job that he is forced to bite his tongue on this occasion.

Settled at last, after the usual muck-up of classes getting into the wrong seats and having to file out into the row behind or in front. I often feel it might be better if they were allowed to choose their own seats, like at the pictures, but tradition dies hard. On the other side of the coin it does mean that we have some control over the company they keep on these solemn occasions.

I turn to the pianist to ask what hymns (songs we call them for the sake of informality) she has chosen first, but realise to my horror that the piano stool is empty. I quickly despatch a runner for Marjory Squires our 'resident pianist'. He returns gasping out that she hasn't arrived at school yet. This is nothing short of a catastrophe! The only alternatives are Roger Goldsmith who repertoire is restricted to *When The Saints Go Marching In*, which we really flogged to death last week when Marjory was off sick, or Joe Johnson.

Now Joe is the finest fellow in the world. He will go out of his way to help anyone anytime. I have never heard a bad word said about Joe. Indeed it's no more than he deserves, as I don't think he is capable of an unkind thought. He is in his mid-fifties and came into teaching after a career in the Merchant Navy and seems to spend most of his time catching up on the years he has missed. I don't say that in any critical way either. He is a fanatically dedicated teacher, not only in lesson times, but his breaks, lunch-hours, evenings, weekends and even holidays are crammed with school activities. He looks after all our visual aids and is always ready to set up some project for a colleague, even if it encroaches even further on his own time. He also runs our Duke of Edinburgh Award scheme single-handed throughout the school and in a host of other ways lends his support to activities that have anything remotely to do with the welfare of the school and its pupils.

How I wish he could play the piano though! How I wish he knew how *terribly* he plays the piano! His playing has been compared to Les Dawson's but I don't think it's that good. I have heard assembly referred to as *Name that Tune* when Joe's at the piano, which seems a bit mean, but it really is that bad. It's a great problem for me, standing out there at the front, trying to preserve some vestige of dignity while the staff are sitting with their heads down, hankies stuffed in their mouths, going purple with the effort of trying to suppress their laughter. As for the kids, they either fall about or simply stick their fingers in their ears, lacking as they do the subtlety of tact.

Meanwhile, Joe has got himself firmly established on the piano stool and is hammering and banging away at the keys as if he's trying to mend a leak. Every tune is liberally sprinkled with duff notes and the whole thing changes key every few bars. But he is in his element. Having rattled off a little something by way of an introduction, we settle for *Lord Of The Dance* as our opener. We sing these 'mod' hymns in assembly, which I think are awful, but the previous head had a thing about them, being a bit of a forward-thinker. He also spent a lot of money on song books for them so we're stuck with them.

Judged by the response from the songsters, they don't think much of them either. The first crack at *Lord Of The Dance* is so ragged that I call a halt after the first line and give them a bit of oratory about making the best of a miserable Monday morning by letting rip with a cheerful song as loud as they can and we're off again.

Unfortunately, this is where another of Joe's little instrumental shortcomings shoots the whole job down. Timing, of course, is crucial to a choir/accompanist relationship and to add to his list of radical problems, Joe plays the piano rather like someone walking across a moor; sometimes he gets bogged down, occasionally he slithers, at times the going is sound and he fairly races along. Alas, all this takes place with total disregard for the singing, with the result that, most of the time, either pianist or singers emerge as clear winners by several bars. Pete Cookland reckons that one day he's going to run a book on the winners of the assembly hymns.

On this occasion, the singers are well ahead in the closing stages but lose their nerve and the performance grinds to a halt like an old-time gramophone record running down.

This is really beginning to get to me. I'm standing here like Bruce Forsyth, trying to flog some enthusiasm into the proceedings, the staff are wetting themselves right, left and centre, and the kids don't know whether to laugh or cry. As for

Joe, he's so gripped with concentration that he's oblivious to the fact that he is on his own again.

On top of all this, I have noticed a group of regular bother-causers starting to show well-known signs of mischief, heads bowed, shoulders bunched and shaking, the whole thing punctuated by occasional snorts of laughter. I could leave them but the waves of disturbance are spreading and attracting more and more attention. I'm afraid that it may be due to Joe's playing and although I don't want his feelings hurt by their apparent thoughtlessness, I have to make a show of authority or risk losing respect.

Thinking back on it, I might have been better saying something like, "Right, whatever's going on over there had better stop now or I'll have you lot afterwards." That could well have put an end to it there and then. What I do say, however, is "What *is* going on in that group on the third row?"

I naturally expect some comment about Joe's playing which I intend to jump on, so I am completely dropped-on by the matter-of-fact answer, "Freddie Morrison's farted," followed by an eruption of laughter right round the hall.

I'm so thrown in fact, that I almost reply out loud, "Oh! That's a relief!" because Joe's feelings have been spared so unexpectedly. Luckily I just manage to fall back on my favourite but usually fatal expletive, "WHAT!" I say fatal because whilst it's meant to convey so much horror and disbelief as to stun the gathering into a shocked silence, I never seem to learn that some nitwit invariably fails to recognise its rhetorical nature and either repeats the question or provides an answer.

On this occasion, Charles Delaney rather in the manner of a court usher, leans over, hand cupped to the side of his mouth, and solemnly but with great glee, kindly informs me, "He says Freddie Morrison's pooped, Sir."

"I *know* what he said. I am just trying to remember if I have ever heard anything like it in my life before and in *assembly* too!"

"You *didn't* hear it did you, Sir?" Charles observes innocently from the wings.

"And will you stop putting your five-pennorth in," I explode finally, turning on him. This third rebuke in such quick time is too much for someone of his volatile nature. Dramatically he leaps up, knocking his chair over, barges past the record player, setting it rocking precariously and slams across to the window. He stands there with his back to us all, glaring out and muttering viciously, though thankfully, inaudibly to me.

I've opened a right can of worms here. I think I'd better get back to the guilty party. "And *you* the captain of the football team." Just where the connection comes I can't quite see, but usually the very thought of being left out of that august band is enough to pull any offender back into line. "Anyway," my last word on the subject, so slowly and with great significance. "If it ever happens again, my lad, I shall make you stand on a chair and give us a SOLO!"

Order more of less restored, much to my relief, I become aware of Joe on my right, raring to go again. "Shall we try *I Gotta Home in Glory Land* next?" he almost begs. "I think that's a bit more lively for a morning like this."

I'd love to have another go if only for Joe's sake, but I feel I've had enough for now. So I spread my arms, palms upwards, "I wish we could really, but we were so late starting and the interruptions haven't helped. I think that if we go on any longer, half the morning will be wasted." Everybody but Joe looks immensely relieved, so after dashing off *The Lord's Prayer* in world-record time, classes start filing out a row at a time.

10:00 am. All but the last handful have left the hall. Roger Goldsmith wants a quick word with me about something or other, but before he can speak, I notice the curtains being twisted into a spiral by a body inside them. Now these curtains are quite an item. They are fully-lined and extend in sections the length of the hall. I am constantly telling children not to mess them about so naturally I'm not very pleased at this latest bit of disobedience. I'm certain that I saw Silly Little Andrew Green sidling towards them so it must be him inside. Silly Little Andrew is easily put back into line by a tap or even a glare, and on this occasion I decide that the former will do me more good as I'm beginning to forget what my right arm is for.

"Excuse me one moment, Mr Goldsmith. I'll just sort this small problem out then I'll be right with you." I step lightly to the curtain and select what I'm sure is the back of the head from the neat, round contour. I give it a mild slap with my palm, but realise from the contact I make with a slight protuberance that I have got my cranial geography wrong, a fact confirmed by an enraged bellow from inside the curtain. I step back in alarm at the violence of the body's efforts to extricate itself from the curtains. When it eventually bursts out, I discover to my horror that it is not Silly Little Andrew Green, but The Dreaded Wayne Lawson, terror of the middle school.

Wayne is the most angelic-looking little boy you could ever hope to see. When my wife saw him at a school fete, in his best clothes, shiny as a new pin, hair immaculate, 'adorable' was her word for him. It was as much as I could do to stop her from taking him home. Not only was he dressed to kill, but also when he came over to talk to us he was on his most charming behaviour and she was quite captivated by his endearing little speech-impediment. He can't pronounce the letter 's'. It always comes out 'f', which makes him sound rather like an ancient Bible, though few of the words in his regular vocabulary would be likely to find their way into any Bible.

Regrettably, the credit side of Wayne's character is rarely seen and when crossed he is a wildcat. He goes berserk! He kicks, scratches, bites, spits, snarls, curses. Indeed, for a ten-year-old and a small one at that, he can be a really nasty proposition in one of these moods.

So you can imagine how my heart sinks when it's Wayne, scarlet with rage and not the innocuous Andrew, who propels himself from the folds of the drapes, out of the hall, down the corridor and through the fire escape doors. These lead out onto the playing field. He races about thirty yards and turns defiantly, fists clenched, ready for anybody. Meanwhile I have followed in his wake, trying to mix speed with nonchalance.

When we eventually come face to face but just out of reach, it is Wayne who takes the initiative. "You've no need to come after me. I'm goin' 'ome."

I pause for a few seconds to decide what course of action to take and conclude that attack is going to be the best form of defence. I am aware that a posse of spectators has crept out behind me and I can't afford to appear to be trying to get round him.

"I've no intention of chasing after you, lad. You've heard me telling people dozens of times about messing about with those curtains so you got what you deserved. Now get yourself back inside to your class."

"Fuck off!"

"What!?" There – I've done it again. When will I ever learn?

"I said fuck off you baftard!"

"I *heard* you the first time."

"Well, wot did yer afk for then? Yer daft or what?"

I'm definitely well behind on points after only one round. I could have him after only a few strides as his little legs don't go very fast, but one thing I will not do is go racing after kids and finish up in an undignified sprawl. I either get them in a position from which they can't escape or they have enough sense to come to me of their own volition.

"Well, I warn you, you either come and face it now or wait till later and the longer I have to wait for you, the worse my temper's going to be. After what you just said to me in front of other people you are *really* in for some pain."

The mention of other people reminds me of the spectators. I round on them and snarl, "You lot should be in your classes by now, not noseying round here – now MOVE IT!"

They scatter in all directions and I turn back to Wayne. He has moved a few yards further away.

"Well, have you decided?"

"I'm ftill goin' 'ome. I'm fick of you. You're alwayf pickin' on me for nowt."

"No, I'm not. You pick on yourself by doing stupid things that you know will only get you into bother."

"Anyway, you're not 'ittin' me. I'm goin' fer me dad. He'll come and fort you out. Even t'polife are fcared of him. *They* call him Mad Mick. Juft you wait till 'e getf 'ere mate."

"Your *dad*! Don't make me laugh. You'll have to find him first. Then you'll have to draw him a map because he won't have the faintest idea where the school is." This is a bit below the belt I know, but I feel that the rule book was thrown out of the window when he started swearing at me in front of all those others – something that really gets to me.

""Right then, I'm off, and you fee if he doefn't come and get you. He'll fmafh yer fafe in." With that blood-chilling threat, he is away across the field and down the drive.

10:15 am. I realise that my lot have simply been left to their own devices so I had better get across to the 'Mansion'. Happily, when I arrive they have had the sense to anticipate what we shall be doing and most of them have made a start.

"I'm pleased to see that you're becoming adult enough to get on with something if I just don't happen to be there to tell you. It goes down well with employers when their workers can be relied on to work on their own initiative. What do I mean by that?"

"What do you mean be what?" queries Peter Howard in his usual abrupt manner.

"Working on your own initiative."

"It means without being telled."

"Told," I correct automatically, though why I do it I don't know because they will always talk that way. I suppose I should feel to be betraying my ideals if I didn't make the gesture. "Good. Correct."

"What if it's wrong what yer doin'?"

"Well obviously you need to be pretty sure you're on the track. If you're in any doubt, what should you do?"

"Ask."

"Right. Remember, if in doubt, always ask. Nobody will ever get cross with you if you ask."

"You do."

"I do not."

"You do."

"WHEN?"

"Sometimes when we're working and you're readin' t'paper and we keep asking questions you get right narky and tell us to shurrup and stop asking daft questions."

"Ah well! Er – yes – well – I mean – I'm probably looking through the paper for important news items so we can all keep up-to-date. When I say *daft* questions I mean that for sure I've already explained something a dozen times and somebody hasn't been listening."

"Oh aye! I bet you're lookin' at page three." General bawdy laughter.

"For your information, know-all, the paper we get, namely the *Daily Express*, has world events on page three, not pictures of naked birds. You'd know that if you ever looked through it as I ask you to. Which reminds me, it's time we were doing our news work."

We get a daily paper, which I think is a most important part of our programme. Most of our pupils are totally ignorant of world affairs when they come into the Leavers' Group as I invariably discover after giving them a brief initial test of current affairs. Now I make a point of spending part of each day, however short that time may be, keeping up with the main items of news.

On Monday mornings I always have ready a large sheet of card on which are pasted numbered pictures of five of the last week's major news stories – one for each day. We discuss each picture in turn then they each write a brief report covering the subject in their own words. We have to have this discussion first or most of them would never be able to even make a start.

"Right then, picture number one. Any offers?" The photo shows two young women smiling from their frames.

"RAPE! THEY WERE RAPED. THESE FELLERS BROCK IN AN RAPED 'EM." Luke beams round triumphantly at his rare success in being first on the button.

"Isn't it marvellous! I bet I could show you a photo of the Queen and you wouldn't recognise her, but anything to do with rape or pornography or sadism—"

"WHAT'S SADISM?"

"That's your homework for tonight. Go home and ask your dad. With any luck he might give you a demonstration."

Bit by bit we piece the information together with contributions from the usual sources. Some of them don't know it's Tuesday till Friday and as for answering questions— By the same process we build up the jigsaw on the protracted love life of the Prince of Wales, Kevin Keegan's match-winning goal for Southampton against Arsenal, and someone even recognises Arthur Scargill, which is a minor miracle. However, by the time we get to picture number five, it dawns on me that most of the answering has been done by Big Arthur, Peter, Jeremy Knight, Christine Major, with an occasional comment from Louise who knows but is too shy to fully join in such discussions. Time for a blast.

"Look – it's been light for nearly three hours yet most of you look as if you're still in bed with the curtains drawn. If you can't be alert on the first morning of the week it's God help us by Friday."

I pick up the remaining photo and walk over to the silent, apparently comatose group furthest away from me. I move close so that they won't have the excuse that they can't see. It is a picture of a man holding a baby. It aroused a lot of interest the week before when we first saw it. The father had given a vital organ to save his infant son's life and I really thought that this one would stick, but apparently not.

"Come on now, you can't leave it all to the same few every time. Alvin?" I ask Alvin Cabot, a West Indian with a booming voice and a laugh to match. Unfortunately the voice is used purely for social purposes and is kept in mothballs during lesson-time. He grins, scratches his head with one extended finger, like Stan Laurel, but remains mute.

"Stuart?" I switch my attention to Stuart Parsons. He is the school goalkeeper and remarkably athletic for an ESN lad. (Nowadays, the term 'ESN' (educationally sub-normal) has been replaced by the more appropriate and sensitive classification 'LD', which stands for 'learning disabilities'.) He lives, eats and breathes football and bicycles. His daily diary contains nothing but an endless round of football matches and cycling trips. Strictly speaking, it would appear that he does *not* in fact eat or sleep, but his physique belies that. When it comes to academic work though, it's a different story. In reply to my question, he just looks stolidly ahead. Seeing as I am passing his table, I knuckle him lightly on the forehead. "Anybody in?" I enquire politely. He twists his head upwards to look at me. "Oh good!" I continue, holding the picture in the palm of my hand. "Excuse me but I am making enquiries about these two people. Do you happen to have seen either of them before?"

"Yes, Sir."

"You *do*. Splendid! Could you tell me who this one is?" pointing to the father.

He hesitates, adjusts his position in his seat, looks meaningfully at his neighbours as if he's about to sign a cheque for a million pounds, and breaks the unbearable tension – "It's a man!"

A gale of laughter shakes the walls. Stuart joins in but modestly, unaware of the real reason for all the amusement but reluctant to be a wet blanket.

I do my Hughie Green bit. "It's a man! Well now isn't that truly wonderful folks, and I do mean that most sincerely folks. Stuart, in his very first speaking part, has actually recognised *a man*! I think we all ought to join in and give him a big hand for that." Whistles and cheers follow, but we must get serious again. I grip the edge of his table with both hands and glare at him. "I KNOW IT'S A MAN YOU TEACAKE BUT I WANT TO KNOW WHAT MAN. DO – YOU – UNDERSTAND?"

"Yes, Sir."

"Super. Who is it then?"

"I don't know, Sir."

"Oh, Gawd! How much does it cost to have a nervous breakdown? I thought you might have just had the slightest idea. Well now – let me see who's left. John Bott, do you know?" Head sakes slowly.

"Martin Sissons, do you?" Pushes lips out and stares into space.

"Walter?"

"What, Sir?"

"Oh never mind! It's past your bedtime anyway. Imtiaz?"

"No Thir." Imtiaz is a Pakistani as you might have guessed. He claims to be sixteen. I put him nearer thirty, but I wouldn't say so out loud. He is a wonderfully cheerful lad, with impeccable if slightly antiquated manners, and completely imperturbable. He has a permanent flashing smile and is another with a rather endearing speech impediment. He's an absolutely smashing lad, though very slow and simple. But of course, that is what the job is all about as they say. He can be a bit wearing at times when his anxiety to do well bubbles over.

"How can you say No Sir?, I haven't asked you anything yet. All I said was Imtiaz. I might have been going to ask you if you wanted a hundred pounds."

"Oh yeth, Thir! I would very like that." His English is a bit quaint at times.

“Yes I bet you would, but do you know anything about this man and this little baby.”

“No, Thir.” His answer is accompanied by the usual radiant smile as if he were giving me the best news in the world.

“So we’re back to where we started. Apart from the ones who are always ready to have a go, and Stuart Parsons with his startling revelation, not one of you seems to have the foggiest idea. What about the girls? OK, Louise and Christina, I know you two will be pretty near the mark, but I want to shift the rust from round the brains of some of these others. Maria?”

Maria Peters, a muscular West Indian girl with a violent temper just grins sardonically and shrugs her shoulders.

“I should have known better than to ask. You have about as much interest in your work as that door. Her lip curls even more and I turn away from her before I’m tempted to say something nasty. I could of course say something similar about quite a few of the others about their work, but it’s this one’s attitude that sets her apart.

“Well, my last hope – Pixie and Dixie.” Dutiful sniggers greet this witticism. Pixie and Dixie, alias Adrienne and Caroline, are so nicknamed because they are inseparable, like the TV celebrities. They always sit side-by-side but turned slightly inwards towards each other so that they are in physical contact at all times, even if only by one knee. They reply in the negative to questions by simultaneously lowering their eyes and remaining silent. In the affirmative, they exchange a long conspiratorial look before one of them offers an answer in a barely-audible voice. On this occasion, lowered eyes and silence complete the inquisition.

There we are. In the end I am forced to resort to acquiring the information via the usual routes. It’s sad, but at least I’ve tried. I’m just about to get them organised with the written side of the exercise when Luke’s dulcet tones intervene – “ARE WE WORKING OVERTIME OR WHAT?”

“I don’t follow you, and would you mind speaking a little more softly or you’ll wake somebody up.”

“IT’S ELEVEN O’CLOCK AND IT’S SUPPOSED TO BE BREAK-TIME AT QUART TO. T’YOUNG ’UNS IS COMIN’ BACK IN.”

“Well, why didn’t you tell me before?”

"AH NIVVER SAW 'EM GO AHT."

"Right then we'll have a break. I need to go over to the staff room anyway."

11:00 am. I intended seeing Roger Goldsmith about Wayne, but the room is empty when I get there, apart from Clive Coburn the deputy-head, who is pouring himself a cup of coffee.

"Want one?"

"Please. One sugar, tiny drop of milk."

"Hear you had trouble with His Lordship this morning."

"Wayne?"

"Who else?"

"A dozen that I could think of, but yes in this case. Anyway, where were you in my hour of need? I haven't seen you till now."

"I had to take the minibus in for its service."

"You're not a bad judge first thing on a Monday morning."

"I was with you in spirit."

"It was your arms and legs I could have done with. I suppose I'd better pop in and see Sheila then to let her know about the fun and games before she hears from somebody else."

"How do you think I got to know? She asked me to have a look round the grounds for him because you were tied up with your class."

"Oh! So I'd better get my rear-end in there right away and plead my case."

The Head's office is only just round the corner so I am there inside a few seconds.

"'Morning, Boss."

"Good morning, Ben." The disarming smile instantly dispels any thoughts of tension and puts things in their right perspective. I always said that I could never work for a woman, but this one is truly the exception. I launch into my explanation or excuse, whichever you prefer.

"Sorry about Wayne. It was clumsy of me but it takes nothing at all to set him off. I suppose I've made it a week's hard labour for Roger now."

Sheila shakes her head in silence for a moment. I wonder whether the gesture is because of me or because of Wayne.

"I don't know what we're going to do with him," she says

eventually. "These outbursts are getting more and more frequent. But you know, Ben, if you could see that home you'd have less need to wonder at how he carries on. His mother lives with this man who knocks her about and hits Wayne whenever he gets within range."

"I see. It must be this Mad Mick he was going on about. I thought there was no man in the house."

"Oh yes! Apparently she got mixed up with him after he left his wife and was living rough. He went to live with her and now she's had enough of him but she can't get rid of him." She pauses as I look heaven-wards. "He gets drunk and breaks things up. She was telling me that last week Wayne had to climb out of the bedroom window to get away from him when he went for him with an axe!"

I recall Wayne threatening me with a visit from this character and tell Sheila.

"I don't think you need worry about that," is the response. "I think he spends the days recovering from the nights."

"Good job! All I need right now is some head-banger like that coming looking for me with a bloodstained axe. Anyway, talking of bloodstains, I'd better get back to my class," I say, suddenly remembering. "I'll call and have a quick word with Roger on the way."

It isn't actually on the way, but I feel I owe it to him to go and see how things are. He has a class which makes the army of Attila the Hun seem like pansies! En route, I have chance to reflect about Wayne. Whilst he was mouthing at me out on the field, I was making plans to hang him by his big toes from a beam in the gym, and kick him in the stomach for a couple of hours if I caught him. However, after hearing what the Head had to say, I think I ought to let him down lightly with just the verbals, but in a way that will not let me down as well.

Roger's room is its usual mixture of the odd child trying to work amidst a clamour from the rest. He believes in them all doing 'their own thing'. Still, everyone to his own taste! I'm just about to bellow a greeting to him, when he looks straight at me then slides his eyes to the right. There, at a table near the window, studying a Lego model with exaggerated concentration, is the lad himself. I go right up to Roger and mutter in his ear so that nobody can catch anything. Wayne is very sensitive about that kind of thing.

"Sorry about him this morning. It wouldn't have happened through choice." I seem to be spending most of this morning apologising."

He shakes his head and shrugs his shoulders, which seems to be the standard acknowledgement of any comment about Wayne.

"He came in right after break. I just made as if everything was normal, told him to get on with something. He's been quiet but you know it's like sitting on a bomb."

"Would you like me to do anything?" I don't want to drop any more bricks, but right has to be done and seen to be done, as the saying goes.

"Well I suppose you ought to have a word with him. He might think he's onto a good thing if we ignore it completely. But *please*—" A week's peace of mind rests on that plea, I know.

I find myself shrugging and head-shaking as well. It must be catching. I loom over Wayne (he really is very small) and he studiously ignores me as he continues to examine his model.

"Wayne." I hope the tone is just right – not threatening, but not wheedling. I might as well be invisible. "Wayne!" The voice carries a bit more authority this time. He lifts the model so that he can see both it and me at the same time without actually having to admit that it's me he's looking at, if you understand.

"I'm gunner get piffed outta me 'ead tonight," he says.

"Eh?" is all I can manage in reply. I'm not ready for this one at all.

"I wiff you'd liffen," he says severely. "I faid I'm gunner get piffed outta me 'ead tonight."

I really must learn to concentrate harder. That's the second time already today that he's had to pull me up about it.

"Oh! Any special reason?" I ask faintly. I suppose I had better go along with him for a while.

"Me bruvver'f comin' 'ome from college today and me mam'f 'avin' a party for 'im tonight."

"Your – brother – is – at – college," the reason for the hesitancy is that my brain is desperately trying to keep abreast of my words and I'm afraid of saying the wrong thing again.

"Yef. He'f at fill—feel—feelol—"

"Theological?" I offer, more in hope than expectation.

"Right. He'f at fillogical college."

"And he's coming home today?" I say, bearing in mind that November is a bit early for the end of term. Out of the corner of my eye, I notice Roger having what looks like a mild fit. Either that or he's trying to stop his false teeth from falling out.

I really must get back to my little charmers but first I must grasp the nettle. In a voice that will reach all the curious, which includes everyone if there's a hint of trouble for someone else, I speak the words that strike terror into so many hearts, but not this one. "Wayne, I want to see you in my room after dinner, and don't miss. Right?"

"Yef, Fir." I am amazed at the simplicity of it and even more at the 'Fir'. That should make it easier (if the mood lasts till dinner-time). As I go out I look at the still-grinning Roger and jerking my head towards Wayne, ask "What was all that about?"

"I'll tell you later – it's a bit complicated," is all I get for now.

11:30 am. When I arrive back in my classroom, grins and furtive glances greet me. Something has been going on but it would take too long to get to the bottom of it. As nobody is unconscious or bleeding and the fixtures and fittings appear to be intact, I decide that it wouldn't be worth the effort. I settle for my knowing look, which is meant to convince them all that I know exactly what the score is. The trouble is that from the one window in our room, I can be seen crossing from one building to the other minutes before I arrive. This of course gives them time to compose themselves before I come through the door.

"We thought you'd gone home," Big Arthur breaks the ice as I re-organise the top of my desk.

"Chance would be a fine thing," I reply.

"Can we come and show you what we've written?" Christina Harlow's request obviously means that she thinks she is on a winner this morning. She is a very attractive, vivacious, West Indian girl. Her cheerfulness first thing in a morning is overwhelming. Yet she is capable of reaching the other extreme in a flash. I have seen her fling lethal objects across the room with real intent. At such times, her bared teeth and flared nostrils make her unrecognisable from her normal bright, smiling self. Her work is much the same. Often it is well set out, interesting and legible. Occasionally, her mind seems to go blank and her work looks like a fireworks display. This time, as I guessed, she is really on song. However, within seconds I am surrounded by six or seven other people, jostling and milling around.

"OK, one at once. You know I can only check one at a time. All the others are just wasting valuable time. Besides, I think one or two people forgot to have a bath or change their socks over the weekend."

It is true that most of the hangers-about do so just for a rest. It is certainly true that some of them do not bathe or change their clothing regularly.

All but Christina reluctantly return to their places. Her work today is easy to correct. She lacks the ability to express herself in anything but the most fundamental English, but her spelling, as I said is usually satisfactory and her writing quite legible, even neat. This as I tell them all regularly, is basically all that matters. We accept that none of them are going to be literary geniuses, so I am happy to settle for basic competence and we work hardest of all at this.

Big Arthur has a different problem from Christina. His style, if we can be so pretentious, is far better than hers, but his spelling is so bad that the concentration needed to read and understand a passage of his writing is enough to give you a headache. A few others fall into this category. I often wonder if it will always be so with them, or if some day there will be a click and everything will fall into place.

Jeremy Knight is a mystery in this respect. He comes from a fine home. Four-bedroomed house overlooking the golf course in *the* part of town; Daddy runs a new Jag, Mummy sounds like Margaret Thatcher. Jeremy has everything he wants or needs, apart from any sign of sense or brain activity. He is always in trouble with the police for petty theft – trifles that can be of no possible use to him. At the same time his academic work reaches the level of about a six-year-old. He brings out today's effort which, as usual, is indecipherable.

"Shall I read it to you as it looks to me?" I ask him.

A look of complete disinterest is the only reaction. He might lose face with Arthur or Peter, the 'big two' as far as he is concerned. He sticks to them like mud to a blanket, but as I see it, they are not too happy with his company. He is bad news, but at the same time he is a useful fall guy for them. In turn, he feels the need to do outrageous things to impress them and so the tenuous relationship limps along. Of course, apparent interest in his work would count as a strike against him, hence the lack of response.

"Well," I persist, "I'll read exactly what you've written."

I have to hold it close to make sure. "Drg cog okg snhig rucg okocog." I see that he is in a 'g' phase. Every so often he seems to develop a fascination for a particular letter which then appears in every word until he tires of it and transfers his affections to another. "There, that's exactly what you've written."

"It i'n't."

"Can you read it yourself then?"

"Course I can."

"OK, go ahead." I pass him the book.

He looks at it; mouth working soundlessly, and at length begins hesitantly. He pronounces the words with the exaggerated emphasis which infants in their first nativity play lay on each word, "It – is – a – woman – and – she –'as – bin – raped – by – them – men." He finishes and looks triumphantly at me.

"Well," I say, completely unconvinced. "You must be writing in code. You have written six words in your book, yet you've used, let me see," and I count the words I have written down on my pad, "twelve words in your translation."

I know that he has acute learning problems and I do sympathise, but to be fair he does little to help himself. His attention is so easily diverted that consistently, or even occasionally intelligible work is a forlorn hope. Even so, when I spend time with him working phonetically on what he says he has written, I find that he does understand what letters correspond to what sounds. He simply will not make the effort to put it all together on his own initiative, and I can't be there every time he has to fill in his tax forms.

I try to intersperse good ones with bad ones (in the academic sense) for marking, so that my own brain doesn't seize up in the process. There is a feeling that progress is being made when you take two in succession who only need the minimum of correction, followed by one whose efforts are like a clapped-out car engine that needs stripping then re-assembling.

Louise has completed five precise, grammatically flawless paragraphs. Often I think she could have held her own in a grammar school but here she is, enjoying the benefits of special education. Whether she could have withstood the emotional pressures or not is another matter. Next comes Stuart Parsons who has managed to write a veritable biography on Kevin Keegan and his goal, but hasn't got round to any of the other topics. What makes understanding difficult in this case is that there is not one punctuation mark in the whole piece, and from the way the words are crammed together, you would think that he had to buy the paper himself. In addition, there are, on average, three spelling mistakes in each word. The thought has crossed my mind more than once that the Secret Service could use him in their work, as there is no way that an enemy power could hope to decipher his scrawl.

I manage to coax Alvin Cabot out to check his progress. I have noticed that he has been riveted to his book all this time, his ballpoint a blur. Yet, when I look at what he has done, there are two and a half lines!

"Alvin," I ask him in amazement. "Your pen has been going like a fiddler's elbow for nearly half an hour and this is all you have produced. How on earth do you manage it?"

He grins and almost tucks his head under his armpit, rather like an imitation of an emu, but says nothing. Not a man to boast about his achievements, our Alvin.

Just as I'm about to call a halt, as I realise that lunch-time has arrived, a noise like a pneumatic drill tells me that Luke is about fed up of waiting to receive attention. Last one then, and out he comes. I peer closely at it but am completely defeated. His work is never brilliant, and always requires a considerable effort on my part to fathom it, but this is something else. I simply cannot understand what he is writing about.

"Come to the sheet and show me which picture you're writing about," I ask him. We walk over to the wall and he jabs his finger at the first picture on the left-hand sheet, whilst I am busy studying the sheet on its right.

"You berk!" I explode. "You've only been doing last week's sheet all this time haven't you?" He snarls something about nobody ever telling him anything, so I carry on. “You know your trouble don’t you? When the brains were being given out, you were busy queuing up for an extra helping of mouth!”

12:00 noon. So the morning ends on a mildly chaotic note but they are nearly all happy as they troop across to lunch. Taking the mick out of Towers is one of the most popular sports in the school, so it came just at the right moment for them. As for me, the end of the morning brings a sigh of relief mingled with regret that, as usual I have not been able to get round to check everybody’s work, in spite of my best efforts.

I give them ten minutes before following them to lunch. The Leavers’ Group have their own corner of the dining room as a privilege, and I usually sit with them. I have developed the art of arriving for lunch just as the last person is being served so that I don’t have to queue. Don’t ask me how I do it – you’ve either got it or you haven’t!

Actually, there is a reason other than an aversion to queuing that makes me want to time my arrival at lunch to a T. It is that the table adjoining the serving-hatch is occupied by ‘The Seven Dwarfs’. They are lovely little characters from the Unit, but their eating habits do not invite the closest scrutiny. Unless they are policed the whole time, which is an impossibility, they scorn the use of new-fangled devices like knives and forks. When they are pinned down to using them, their motor-control is not terribly well developed with the result that the ultimate destination of the food is unpredictable to say the least.

I am a bit late today and by the time I arrive, the seven have already received their sweet course. It is rice pudding, so their table looks as if they have had the decorators in.

“Missa Bailey!” one of them shouts gleefully as he spots me, generously sharing his mouthful of pudding with the rest of the table. Seven little mouths, full of rice pudding also, open to give me a delighted grin. Well—six mouths actually. Winford Sleight is on the point of spooning the mixture into his mouth when he receives the wonderful news of my arrival. His mouth turns to greet me, whilst the hand with the spoon in it goes through the routine of food-injection with the result that the rice pud finishes up in his left ear.

Their devotion to me is quite touching because all I ever seem to manage in return is an oafish smirk and a twiddle of the fingers in their direction. Still it seems to make them more than content.

I see from the menu that the first course is 'Savoury Mice'. (The cook has missed an 'n' in case you are wondering). Accepting a sizeable dollop from each tureen in turn, I select the table with the most tolerably-mannered occupants. After the first mouthful I begin to wonder whether in fact the cook has left the 'n' out. To be fair though, whilst this is not my favourite dish, the food is usually very good.

I never have a sweet for weight reasons (mine, not the pudding) so I am quickly through my plateful and ready for a quick excuse-me and away to catch up on a few chores.

12:30 pm. First stop the staff room. I pass the Head on her way out to the playground and briefly fill her in about Wayne. As we part in different directions she calls out, "By the way, Happy Birthday," and moves on chuckling. It takes a moment to sink in then click!

"Oh yes!" I call out after her, "I'll remember next time you're looking for a silly b—"

In the staff room I buttonhole Roger. "Now then what's all this tripe about theological college?"

"Oh your face! I nearly peed myself," he says between snorts of laughter. "No, seriously, what's happened is that the Lawsons have moved from out in the wilds near Netherbridge to an old house near the town."

"So what's that got to do with theological college?" I ask, no wiser.

"Hang on, I'm coming to that. Out at Netherbridge, Wayne and his two brothers used to terrorise the village."

"Doesn't sound much like good vicar material to me," I rudely interrupt again. I am keen to hear the tale, but I have other things to do and he doesn't seem to be getting any nearer to the point.

"That's just it. In fact, the two brothers are inside. The younger one's at a borstal, and the other's been in Walton for a year. He's the one who's coming out today – hence the 'piff-up' tonight."

"Oh!" That news certainly bounces like a leg-break. "But the college bit's still as clear as mud."

"Well—you've got to feel sorry for the mother. She's got these three baskets causing havoc all over the place until they're practically run out of town." He pauses to see if the mists are clearing which they certainly are not in my case. Thankfully, a glance round at the faces of the few others in the room who have also plugged into this fascinating saga, tells me that they are registering zero as well. "So she gets this house just outside town where nobody knows them and invents a story about the sons being at theological college."

"What a load of garbage," I jeer, still not sure whether he's making it all up. "Why couldn't she just keep quiet about them or say they were working away?"

"Oh come on! You've got to remember that the poor woman's as dim as a Toc H lamp herself. I fancy some of the new neighbours are a cut above the Lawsons and she simply wants to get off to a good start."

He obviously means it, but I should have known that Roger wouldn't joke about something like that. In spite of the rich vein of humour that runs through him, he is basically a very serious person, particularly where his work is concerned. His straggly beard and gaunt features give him the appearance of the confirmed zealot. He would be prepared to see good in anybody, even if they had just chopped off both his legs.

1:00 pm. Better get back to HQ. I usually split lunch supervision half-and-half with Mary. I have my break first then take over when I have had something to eat. I notice that her car is not in the park so she must have gone into town. I wonder what might have happened during the short time that neither of us is on patrol. It's hard to think that all these people are (officially) due to become adults in a few months' time. Heaven help the outside world!

As I am unlocking my office door, I hear strange noises coming from along the corridor. It sounds like someone being strangled or asphyxiated sort of 'Urgh—! Argh—! Yergh—!' Alarmed, I dash off in the direction of the sounds to find some of Mary's squad reeling about, clutching their throats, holding their noses, retching and gulping, all pointing towards the little room at the end of the passage.

"What the blazes is going on?" I bawl at them. If they had been in genuine distress they would surely have paid little attention to me. As it is, they scuttle away to their room like cockroaches caught in the light.

As the last of them disappears round the corner, I realise that I have not had the sense to find out what the trouble is all about. However, what is obvious is that it has something to do with the little room in the corner, which happens to be the only upstairs toilet.

Fearlessly I push open the door, already ajar, and boldly enter. I immediately find myself reacting in precisely the same manner as the kids I have just been blasting. Clutching my mouth, I stagger backwards out of the door and lean against the wall gasping for air. The whole action from entering to leaving cannot have taken more than five seconds, but it's amazing what can be taken in visually in such a short time, especially in such a small space.

What I have taken in is an impression that someone has intended to use the toilet, had a change of mind, climbed onto the ceiling and exploded! It's everywhere! Around the bowl, on the floor, in the sink and on the towel. There is also a garland of toilet paper; originally white but now stained a variety of shades, strung between all these points. It looks as if the room has been trimmed up early for Christmas.

As I am recovering my composure, the abrasive sounds of Little Albert and Savage Beast returning from their safari reach me. I feel too nauseated even to cower away from Savage Beast's gargling efforts to get his teeth into my leg. I must look a bit off-colour because Little Albert asks very solicitously if I'm all right. I just nod in reply.

Oh no! Little Albert! I MUST get it cleaned up before he sees it or there will be all hell let loose. He seems to hold me personally responsible for everything that goes wrong in that building but I suppose that is the price of fame. Luckily he appears to suspect nothing and continues on his way dragging the unwilling Savage Beast upstairs to the flat.

Doing a fair impersonation of John Cleese in top gear, I spring along to Mary's room. I burst in and find myself confronted as usual by what looks like the aftermath of a nuclear attack. Debris of all sorts litters the floor and tables. Obviously it is the result of a throwing match across the room as can be judged by the expressions of unnatural innocence as I burst in.

"RIGHT!" I scream, stamping my feet and clenching my fists (even more like Cleese). "WHO'S DONE IT?"

"Done what, Sir?" enquires Ian Welsh sympathetically.

"YOU KNOW WHAT LAD. YOU WERE ONE OF THE GANG WHO RAN AWAY JUST NOW."

Oh that's different! Realising that they have been recognised but unwilling to name the culprit outright, they begin with the eyes. I watch every pair of eyes look up, look down, then round in circles before simultaneously focussing on – Kermit!

Kermit is sitting there gazing into what space is visible beyond his opaque lenses, blissfully unaware that he has suddenly become the centre of attention.

"KERMIT!"

"Yes, Sir," he replies with complete peace of mind.

Aware that I am still raging, I turn down the volume. Either way is all the same to Kermit, so I might as well give my lungs an easy ride.

"Kermit," I continue in a less savage tone. "It *was* you who made that disgusting mess in the toilet, wasn't it?"

"Yes, Sir," he answers proudly, nodding his head emphatically lest anyone should doubt it. Fame at last!

"Kermit – when you use the toilet, you are supposed to sit on the seat not swing from the light-fitting. How on earth did you manage to get it all over the place like that?"

"I gotter upset stomach, Sir," he says with great dignity.

"So have a few others that I could name now," I remark dryly. "But what are we going to do about it? It has to be cleared up before afternoon school starts. That gives us less than ten minutes."

"I clean it up, Sir," says Kermit making a move for the door.

"No thank *you*, Kermit," I tell him grabbing him by the shoulder which seems to be the only part of him free of damp bits and blobs of one kind or another. "I've seen your attempts at cleaning up already."

My eyes wander from one to another, but each refuses to be mesmerised into the task. Thankfully, before my gaze comes to rest on his, Ian Welsh pipes up, “I’ll do it, Sir.”

Now Ian Welsh is many things. His family history and his own present form-sheet suggest that much of his future leisure-time will be spent walking round an exercise-yard. However, give him anything from a cartful of human vomit to a ten-foot pile of manure to sort out and he has few equals on this earth.

1:30 pm. Off they go to spend the afternoon with other members of staff doing ‘vocational work’ which seems to cover everything from sex education to the Highway Code.

My timetable for the afternoon says ‘free’. That is rather like saying that someone sentenced to life for murder instead of being hanged, has been acquitted. I always use this time for catching up. I wish I could say that I am ever successful in that aim, but I fear it will never be so. When one considers that my duties officially embrace the leavers’ class, careers, boys’ discipline, physical education, games, and the maths syllabus, it is hardly surprising. Not that I am complaining – far from it. I can truthfully say that I am never bored! The job reminds me of the music-hall act in which the performer attempts to keep six plates spinning simultaneously at the top of six long poles. The only difference is that he is normally successful.

I decide to start near home and work across to the ‘Barracks’ where I have some phone calls to make. First a walk round the top floor to make sure that all is well. Ian Welsh, invested with all the paraphernalia of the bog-cleaner, is on cloud nine. I know that he will take a big chunk out of the afternoon to do the job, but if it gives him a sense of vocation, it will be well worth it. There is nobody skulking in the many hiding places which are a feature of the ‘Mansion’, so I take a quick look down the cellar to check that the newspapers are still neatly stacked and nobody has been messing about down there. I even have a brief listen to make sure the boilers are firing. I do this because a few weeks ago Little Albert was going into orbit over some joker who kept creeping down the cellar and switching them off. Of course people complained and Albert in turn bent my ear until it stopped. Whether or not this was connected with the dire threats I made to the culprit in assembly is a matter of conjecture.

Going across to the 'Barracks', I remember – Wayne! He never showed up at lunchtime so I had better call there first.

It's obviously on his mind, because before I can say a word, he runs to meet me and blurts out, "I waf there, Fir. Af foon af I finiffed me dinner I came and you never turned up. Then I 'ad to come back 'ere when the bell went like Mr Goldfmiff fayf."

"All right, Wayne. You did the right things and it's my fault that I never saw you. BUT I still need to talk to you, so see me at break this afternoon."

"Aw, Fir!" he protests. "We're playin' a game at break and I'm in it. I'll miff it if I've to come and fee you."

I am bound to agree. "Fair enough then. You don't have much time at break but you do at lunchtime so make it tomorrow at the same time instead. Understand?"

"Yef, Fir."

He says this last bit so humbly that I walk out of the room feeling really powerful and in command, knowing that all the others in that class saw it as well which is equally important. Things have a way of balancing out in this job though, one minute you're in command, the next you can be struggling to stay on your feet.

A breathless youth hails me. "I've been looking all over for you, Sir. You're wanted on the telephone. It's a woman," he adds with a leer.

"Thanks. I've been hiding in the cellar."

From the look he gives me as I quicken my step, he obviously thinks I'm cracking up.

"Hello," says the voice at the other end of the phone. "Mr Bailey? You don't know me. I'm Josie Milburn. I'm a probation officer." Her delivery is like a railway engine shunting. She talks as if she is used to being interrupted. I think she is expecting me to comment on the facts so far, but it all seems fairly self-explanatory so I keep quiet and she carries on. "I'm Arthur Davis's Probation Officer."

"Oh dear!" I am roused into comment at last. "I didn't know he was in trouble." I am aware that he did have a stormy passage in his latter days in secondary school, but since he came to us he has been as agreeable as one could wish. I always have a feeling that there is something volcanic about him, but at the moment it is certainly in a dormant state.

"Oh no! He isn't in any trouble at the moment," she continues. "I'm just ringing to see if everything is going well. Actually he is supposed to see me periodically but it's some time since he called in so I thought I had better check. It also gives me chance to introduce myself to you and hope that I can count on your co-operation with him."

"You can certainly count me in," I tell her. "As a matter of fact Arthur is doing really well here. Everybody respects him and he can cope with the work. Never absent, never late, he's just fine as far as we're concerned." I could go on at far greater length but I think the summary sufficient. Besides, I want to hear rather than tell so I press on. "By the way, Mrs Milburn, what did Arthur do to get the wrong side of the law?"

"Oh just a bit of petty larceny. Him and his elder brother and a friend. The two older ones stole goods from the place where the brother worked. Arthur was mainly the look-out, but of course he got roped in just the same."

"It's a pity because he's got more job potential than almost anyone else we've got," I say, hoping to build up a store of credits for him should he ever be in need again. "In fact, he has a tentative offer of work at Smith's when he finishes school in July."

"Oh that's super!" For the first time, her tone betrays something more than friendly but very professional interest in 'the case'. "I'm so pleased that there are a few of us together on this one because there won't be much help from home. Father has washed his hands of him and Mother just rants and raves at him. There are seven in the family, but for some reason he seems to get the blame for everything."

"I understand perfectly. Leave it to me and thank you for calling. Goodbye."

"Thank you. Goodbye."

I must make a point of telling him as soon as possible or it will sink without trace into the swamp of my memory. First though I shall have to ring Sykes's Pickles to arrange a visit for the Leavers. I have drawn a blank with them so far, which is unusual, as they are normally delighted to host us. They probably still are, but we just haven't been able to get our act together yet.

I dial the five digits and wait an age until the office girl finishes filing her nails.

"*Good* afternoon – Sykes's Limited. Pickle Manufacturers. Can I help you?" I'll give her her due. She really makes it sound as if she has been waiting all day just to hear my voice.

"Good afternoon. Ben Bailey, Lees Bank Special School. I've been trying to arrange a visit for our Leavers' Group for some time now. Would it be possible to suggest some dates?"

"One moment, Sir. I'll put you through to Mr Sykes. Who do you say is calling?"

"Ben Bailey, Lees Bank Special School. I know Mr Sykes – we've been to the works several times before."

"Are you a pupil or one of the staff?"

Is she serious? "I'm the senior master love, but I'm flattered that I must sound so young."

"It's not that. Only when adults ring up they usually say it's Mr So and So—"

"I see. I always feel a bit pompous announcing myself as Mr, so I use my first name."

I must have passed the test because after a few blips and squeaks a mellifluous voice says "Hellooo—Mr Bailey, Norman Sykes speaking." (Either a man of class or his secretary has been saying things to him.) "What can we dooo for yooo—?"

This of course is *the* Mr Sykes of Sykes's Pickles, an old-established family business dating back to around the turn of the century. He is a youngish man but something of an antique in his speech and manners, the result maybe, of having greatness thrust upon him at a very early age. His diction is so rounded and precise, that he sounds rather like a male version of the speaking clock. Nevertheless he is very co-operative with the school and can always be relied on to provide an interesting tour of the works.

I greet him warmly because of this and because I know he likes to think of himself as one of our benefactors. "Hello, Mr Sykes, nice to speak to you again. I've rung a few times to try and fix up our annual visit, but so far without luck."

"Yerss, yerss. Jerst wern moment please. I'll consult the daary." I hear the pages rustling. "Yerss, here we aah. How about this coming Thursday? I believe Thursday is your customary visiting day is it not?" Without waiting for a reply he carries on, "2:00 pm suit hmm—?"

"Yes, yes, fine. Thank you, Mr Sykes. Look forward to seeing you then. Bye."

2:30 pm. I end the conversation a bit abruptly. I hope Mr Sykes is not offended, but as I glance out of the office window I see Big Arthur padding across the yard. Looking down at my watch I realise that it is now afternoon break and I have spent a complete half-session on these calls. This happens continually but people refuse to believe that such things can be so time-consuming.

I knock on the window to attract Arthur's attention and dash off to catch up with him seeing as I intend going in his direction. He is standing sideways on to me as I catch up with him, stooping and with his long arms dangling loosely at his sides. I try to suppress a smile as the Pink Panther tune ghosts through my mind, but he notices and returns the imagined greeting with his usual non-committal half-smile, which glimmers but quickly disappears.

"I've been talking to a friend of yours on the phone – Mrs Milburn. The half-smile, which I am sure is more of a nervous than a motor reaction, returns. "She says she'd like to see you again any time you feel like dropping in."

The half-smile flickers, he nods briefly, but gives nothing away. It's impossible to tell whether or not he has seen behind the casual message.

I was intending to go up to my office and have a coffee, but as we are about to pass the end of the strip of tarmac that divides the courtyard from the playground, I notice the unmistakeable sign of trouble. A crowd is gathering round a spot just inside the playground and others are approaching like iron filings to a magnet.

"Aye-aye! Trouble on the port beam. See you lads later. Don't forget Mrs Milburn will you, Art?" Without waiting to test the reaction this time, I approach the crowd. On these occasions I try never to hurry as this only causes alarm so that by the time you get there, the birds have flown.

I spot one small area where the ranks have not yet closed and nip to the front. The surface on which the school is built is almost entirely clay. Because of this we are plagued, in wet weather by a large number of puddles of various sizes and depths and it is around one of the largest of these that the flock has gathered. It is not the puddle that is the main source of attraction though, but a set of four lads known to all as 'The Black Hand Gang', for obvious reasons. They are forming up in a line and running across the puddle. To prevent them from landing in the water, which is very wide, they are using as a stepping-stone what appears to be a bulky sack. On closer inspection however, the 'sack' can clearly be seen (and heard) to be making efforts to climb out of the puddle only to be flattened again as the jumpers keep up their momentum.

By now the spluttering and gurgling from the wretched object in the puddle are taking on a desperate edge. The shrieks of morbid delight from the onlookers are becoming tinged with anxiety. I have seen enough not to be caused any tremors of doubt by barefaced denials from the four villains, so I step in.

"THAT'S ENOUGH!"

Everybody of course whirls round at the sound of the voice and the four stop dead in their tracks. The object of their attentions, meanwhile, staggers to its feet and I have a chance to identify it. "Oh no! Not you again." As I said before, any attention is better than none – that's right – it's Kermit!

"Yessir," he assures me, belching out yellowish water, which is also cascading from the top of his head all the way down his saturated clothing and back into the puddle. Worse still, I realise as he bends and begins groping around in the filthy water, that he has once again lost his specs.

Furious, I turn to the gang. "You miserable, useless, brainless IDIOTS!" By verbally savaging them to start with, I am hoping to dissipate some of the anger which will inevitably burst all over them when I take hold of the cane in a few minutes' time. "I have never seen anything more stupid or cruel in my life—"

As I pause and feel around for more words to hurl at them, Raymond Jankowicz (as black as coal in spite of his name) explains with a bright smile, "We was jus' playin' a game with him, Sir."

"Playing a game. Playing a GAME! What was it called – sink the Titanic?" I feel that such penetrative wit deserves more than the puzzled looks it receives.

"No, Sir. It dint 'ave no name. We jus' made it up," explains Raymond.

"What about you other three? What have you to say for yourselves, eh?" Nothing apparently, just blank looks. "You *really* look as if you've enjoyed it," I say to Kermit who is still sifting the contents of the bottom of the puddle in an attempt to find his glasses.

"Hergh—hergh—hergh—" Kermit beams radiantly with sound effects. "OK then, I tell you what," I go on. "We'll *all* play a game. You," pointing to Kermit, "have had all the fun so far so you can't join in this one. You can go to Nurse Thomas and ask her if she can find you something to wear till your own clothes have dried. You others can come with me and we'll have *lots* of fun. What happens is that I have this big stick and I see how much dust I can get out of the seats of your pants." The whites of their eyes are by now showing up very clearly against their dark faces.

2:45 pm. End of break. Kermit has gone for repairs and I am holding the four culprits back until the rest of the school has gone back inside. I don't like to make a public spectacle of this kind of thing. It takes a little time for the last of them to dribble through the doors and by this time the four have begun to shiver a little from a mixture of apprehension and the cold air. I have been warmer myself, but it's all part of the build-up.

Eventually we troop solemnly into school and make our way to the hall past the last person left in the junior cloakrooms. I install the condemned quartet in a quiet corner of the hall, six feet apart, to heighten the sense of drama, then go for my thrashing tackle. I usually talk about 'the cane' but rarely use it. I feel that it is too much part of a primitive and barbaric past. Instead, I root out an old training shoe with a heavy-duty patterned sole, which is more than sufficient for the purpose as a rule.

Before sentence is carried out, I say a few words designed to remind them of why we are here. That may sound odd but it is not beyond the bounds of possibility that, by now, they might have forgotten how it all started. As I speak I hold the training shoe in my right hand and tap it lightly but menacingly against the palm of my other hand.

"That was the meanest, most unfeeling *and* dangerous – don't forget how cold it is out there – thing I have seen for a very long time—" I begin.

"Sir, we was only 'avin' a joke wiv 'im," Raymond breaks in with a last desperate bid for a reprieve.

"It might have been a joke to you, sunshine," I resume, jabbing him in the chest, "but it didn't seem to be doing much for Jeremy did it? Oh no! I'm not buying that one." I use Kermit's proper name to add emphasis to the fact that the 'joke' has completely lost its credibility. "Right, that's enough yap. It'll be one each this time seeing as you seem to have been going straight lately. BUT—let me see one of you for the wrong reason within the next few weeks and you will really come in for some agony."

Only one it is, but I really lay it on. Truly I don't enjoy it, but sadistic as it may sound, I always have difficulty keeping my face straight afterwards. The physical and facial contortions that follow a hefty slap on the behind always seem to me to have a certain slapstick amusement. On the serious side, there is the satisfaction of knowing that the intended effect has been achieved without the possibility of physical damage. A poke in the eye with a very sharp stick or a blow over the head with a metal bar would be a different thing altogether.

I keep my eye on them as they crawl painfully away round the corner to their classroom just to make sure that they don't take anything out on the doors or windows.

So to Kermit. As I approach the main corridor, Rachel Thomas, our Nurse, comes briskly to meet me, obviously none too pleased.

"Ooh, I could kill you!" is her somewhat discouraging greeting. "I've just finished giving some of the little ones their injections and there has been a stream of accidents all afternoon. Now you send me this dozy ha'porth just as I'm going to have a breather and a cup of tea."

"Well that's a nice welcome I must say, Florence." I call her Florence just to irritate her, mainly when she is already peeved.

"I'm just trying to make sure that you don't get bored and all I get for my trouble is abuse. Where is he anyway?"

"In there," she jerks her head impatiently towards the medical room. "He's as daft as a brush. If I was his mother I'd have put him down."

"Really, Florence. You'll have to give that lamp some polish. It's starting to get dull."

With another disgusted snort, she goes into the staff room. I open the door of the medical room where Kermit is standing, still in his sodden clothes. By now, he is a delicate shade of blue and his teeth are emitting a noise like someone playing the spoons.

"What on earth are you doing still in those wet clothes you clown?"

"I abn't got no more, Sir."

I dash off into the staff room to Nurse. "He's still in his wet clothes and his teeth sound as if they're doing a tap-dance."

She puts down her teacup with elaborate dignity and regards me, her lips pressed together. "Well he will be till he gets some more," she says acidly.

"I asked him to ask you if you would find him some."

"Well he never told me that, the dateless article. He said you were going to see to him."

"I've nothing at all just now," I protest. "The football kit is still in the drier from the last game. Can't you find him something for now?"

"Oh all right. I'll have a look but I don't know what I've got. You know what it's like on wet days."

"Thanks, love. While you're doing that I'll make him some tea or he's likely to die from exposure."

"It'll take more than a wetting to harm that great slack lump."

"You know, Rachel, you're beginning to make me think you don't like our Kermit."

"It's not that. I feel sorry for the poor kid but he's that *daft*. Still there wouldn't be much point in him being here if he was a hundred per cent I suppose."

I make her sound a bit of a dragon, but really she is the ideal woman for the job. Her background is a military one and she uses it to good effect when the occasion demands. On the other hand she can easily spot a genuine case. Thanks to this happy combination we manage to avoid the kind of panic stations that can put the fear of God into everyone.

Whilst she goes off to minister to Kermit's needs, I wait for the kettle to boil. When it eventually obliges, I pour him a cup of sweet, milky tea.

When I get back to the medical room with the tea, Kermit's clothes are steaming on the radiator. The lad himself is by now dolled-up in a blouse made for a very big girl, not Kermit's scrawny torso, a pair of girls' navy-blue knickers and tights, and enormous wellies.

"Good grief! He looks like a principal boy," I say to Nurse. Wasn't there anything else?"

"Beggars can't be choosers," she replies with a wicked grin and I know that she has done it on purpose. I have to hand it to her though; it's the sort of example that ensures that we don't have many malingerers.

"Well, I'm going to spoil it for you," I say in retaliation. "I'm not sending him back to his class looking like a dog's dinner. He'll have to stay in here."

"If I have any more patients he'll have to stand in the corridor. It might be a girl."

I have a horrific vision of an inspector or one of the school governors calling out of the blue and being confronted by this apparition. They could be affected for life.

Meanwhile, Kermit's teeth have stopped chattering and he is making terrible rasping noises instead. Alarmed, we both rush to him.

"What's the matter – what is it, Kermit?"

"Aargh—! Grgh—!"

"What *is* wrong?"

"I not like sugar in my tea, Sir."

"Oh for goodness sake! Is that all? Get it down your neck; it will make you feel better. I'm sorry we don't have any whiskey to put in it for you."

"Hergh—hergh—hergh—" The idea obviously appeals to him.

3:15 pm. About this time each day, the buses arrive and park up ready for the journey home. If I am free, I go out and help Bob Robins. He is a big, genial, Kentish man. The father of seven grown-up children, he is nevertheless permanently bristling with energy and good nature. I really don't know how he always manages it. He is another of our staff with a military record. He makes use of it in the bluff, vigorous way in which he runs the woodwork and metalwork departments. He is therefore just the man to organise the exacting business of making sure that over two hundred pupils get on the right bus to go home.

The buses are staffed by drivers and escorts, but the drivers are there only to drive and the escorts to supervise inside the vehicles. Because of this it is imperative that there are members of the teaching staff to supervise the rest of the operation. It all sounds relatively simple, but believe me, it is more than one man's work, even for one like the capable Robert.

Today, all the transport is in good time, so I go around the doorways and hiding places clearing out the loiterers. It's amazing how the last quarter of an hour is just fifteen minutes too long for a regular band of pests to hang around their favourite haunts on all manner of pretexts. Their excuses vary from the call of nature to looking out for the buses so that their teacher does not run the risk of several minutes overtime.

Shakila is one of these. She is a great obstinate bulk of a girl. For the umpteenth successive day I approach her like Dixon of Dock Green with the familiar, "Right, Shakila, move along there please. No loitering in the corridors if you don't mind. Back to your class till we're ready for you."

As usual she staunchly contends, "Mr Cookland, he say to look out for buses."

I counter with the standard reply, "Tell Mr Cookland, Mr Bailey he say you get on bike back to classroom pretty damn quick or you get boot in awkward place." There follows the rest of the ritual conversation as I lead her by her muscular arm back to her class. In it, she threatens me with a visit from Father, who is king of their community (when he is not on nights,) Mother, sisters, brothers (one of whom does kung-fu,) Uncle (who has a knife,) and the rest of the family too numerous to mention. I remark how charming it will be to meet such intriguing people. Thus we pass the journey in good-natured discussion before I open her door and propel her into the room.

Back then to empty the toilets (not literally of course). Pupils left in there for any length of time find that they have remarkable gifts for making things like radiator valves work in unusual ways, like producing floods of water all over the floor. They also discover facts like standing on the lavatory seat makes it easier to look out of the window and see the buses arrive, but it also tends to have a shattering effect on the lavatory pan and produces even more spectacular floods of water. The regulars are in there today so I speed them on their way with a few unconvincing growls and half-hearted threats.

3:30 pm. Out they pour, a class at a time, little ones first. The drivers like to be away by 3:40 pm so we try to oblige in order to keep the peace. The little ones are no problem. They file slowly but obediently aboard, chattering happily, waving goodbye to friends and teachers.

It's when we reach the senior school that we get problems. The Leavers go at 3:20 pm to avoid the rush. They travel by public transport as part of their social training. They are rarely any bother, as to lose this privilege would be a disgrace for them. No, it's the two or three classes below them who generally cause the problems, and try as we may, it's a rarity for us to have them all away before the deadline. Sometimes a whole class will be held back, other times it may be a small group or even an individual who causes the hold-up.

Fights and feuds are fewer on the journey home, and it is mainly, to be honest, staff who are the cause of last-minute hitches. As their patience wears thin at the end of the day, they tend to indulge in petty obstructiveness like keeping everyone waiting until one little nuisance finally decides to toe the line.

So far the going is encouragingly smooth right down to the end. Right to the very end! Right to the last *one* in fact! The Head, who usually takes charge of matters at the school end, is about to give us a thumbs-up to send them away, when a messenger from within causes her to change to the 'wait' signal instead. She calls out something inaudible to go with it.

"Pardon?" I enquire.

"Just – one – more!" through cupped hands.

"Oh shit!" through clenched teeth whilst simultaneously waving acknowledgement.

For minutes, which start to feel like hours, we wait. Frustration can be heard mounting on board the buses. Finally, out of the main door stagger two figures. I can't make out what the situation is. Vanity alone prevents me from wearing my glasses, even though someone did tell me they look sexy, so at the moment the whole thing is blurred. At first it looks like a courting couple, arm in arm, but as they come closer, it is evident that they are the same sex and are exchanging words, though not it seems with any venom. It is hard to tell whether one is supporting or escorting the other. A little further and it becomes clear that one is large, portly, and adult, whilst the other is skinny, short, and juvenile. A few more strides and they are identifiable. It's Joe Johnson and Charles Delaney.

It is all clear now. Each has obviously tested the other's patience to the limit during the day but they are still going through the motions of the age-old battle for dominance, oblivious of everyone else on the scene. Charles is dishevelled, his collar sticking up round his enormous ears like an Elizabethan ruff. Joe is puffing, his suit is rumpled, and his normally immaculate RAF hair has allowed a quiff to escape and dangle across the bridge of his nose. The tattered remnants of their argument are just about audible as they approach the steps of the bus.

"Gerroff yer fat cunt!" says Charles, totally without malice.

"Shaddap and get on the bus," replies Joe in his Stepney Green accent, completely unoffended, as he gives Charles a gentle shove up the steps. I have to turn away so that nobody can see me laughing. That final little piece of action about sums it up for me.

3:45 pm. Peace at last! I've heard it said and it's true I'm sure, that it's harder to get away from school at the end of the day than it is to get there in the morning. I usually spend some time at the end of the day either in preparation or reparation, but today I just wait for the signal from my brain to be received by my legs. I am sitting in the staff room finishing a cup of coffee, letting other peoples' conversations waft over me. At last the urge comes and I push myself out of the chair.

"That's enough for me for one day," I tell anyone who might happen to be listening. "You lot can stay here all night if you like but that is definitely my lot for this day."

I always feel a bit guilty if I go home before the others, but today is an exception. As I pass through the doorway I almost collide with Clive Coburn. "See you later then," he says.

"Yep. See you tomorrow."

His Father Christmas laugh gives me the sinking feeling that maybe something has slipped my memory.

"Don't tell me you've forgotten?" he says in mock-horror.

"Forgotten?" I echo faintly.

"The Parent-Teacher Association meeting – every second Monday."

I don't need to make any rapid calculations to know that tonight's the night. "Aw fff—flamin' heck! I eventually manage, to my eternal credit.

Continuing the homeward trudge, I hear my name being called, I turn back towards the staff room to see a hairy paw waving at me and a noise-like singing "Happy birthday to you, happy birthday to you—"

TUESDAY

12th November

9:10 am. I am in my office overlooking the drive. It is a beautiful day, more like the return of summer than autumn. The postman looked good today in his lightweight uniform, striding jauntily along without a care.

Last night was frantic. In addition to the PTA meeting, there was our monthly Cricket Club meeting which I had also forgotten. This meant that I had to leave the PTA in order to put some time in at the other one. Actually it was no great hardship as Kermit's parents were at the former demanding to know why he had arrived home looking like one of the Three Musketeers, and with one lens of his specs missing. It turned out to be a case of 'out of the frying pan' though. I exchanged the inquisition of one for the deadly boredom of the other. Our Cricket Club meetings are an endless drag of disputes over the state of the ladies' toilets and the reasons for the delay in digging the drains for the new showers. I spent the sleeping part of the night dreaming of Kermit stuck in a drainpipe into which he had gone in search of his specs. As a result, I am feeling a little fragile this morning.

My thoughts are cut short by the roar of the buses up the drive. There is something awesome, warlike, about this ritual. I think it has something to do with their size and speed, and the din they make in the confined, echoing space. This morning, as the surge of bodies from them thins out, I spot a figure doing something at, or to, the back of one of the vehicles. Time to go into action.

I hurry downstairs and across the drive. He is so engrossed that he is unaware of my approach. He is bending over, writing a slogan in the grit covering the paintwork, with his finger. They have been told a hundred times not to do this because of the damage it causes, but this young man obviously feels that he is immune from such restrictions. His name is Tony Bath, a proper little know-all. He is a pleasant-looking lad from the middle school, smartly dressed, his rimless spectacles giving him the appearance of an embryo accountant or solicitor. Unfortunately, as I say, he's a real pain. He is never wrong, disagrees on principle with anything and everything and will never agree that there may be a better way of doing a thing than the one he knows.

Armed with this knowledge, therefore, I have no hesitation in booting him firmly in the backside which is conveniently extended for the purpose as he bends to his composition on the back of the bus. Unhappily, instead of jerking upright as they usually do in the circumstances, he overbalances and smacks the top of his head on the metal, causing his executive specs to clatter onto the gravel.

He clutches his head with one hand and picks up his glasses with the other, turning wrathfully on me. "You've damaged my spectacles and they cost nearly fifty pounds," he pronounces, squinting indignantly in my direction.

"Just come down here with me and we'll find out how much you owe the bus company for damage to this bodywork," I say, ignoring his reprimand. We walk to the open door of the coach and look up at the driver who is in his seat, reading the paper. "How much do you reckon it will cost to respray the back of your bus?" I ask, winking at him.

He sees the lad and knows the score straight away, as it is a well-worn routine. "About five hundred quid I should think," he answers, thoughtfully rubbing his cheek and frowning.

"Huh! You could do that job in ten minutes with a bit of rubbing compound and some clean cloths," says the professor scornfully.

"Shut up, Einstein!" I snap at him. "Tell you what," I say returning to the driver, "would you settle for hanging on another five minutes whilst this young man washes the whole of the back end and not just the bit he's written on?"

"Champion," chuckles the driver. "Somebody has it to do and that's usually me so it'll suit me fine."

“Have you got five hundred to spare?” I ask the boy, who simply looks away disdainfully. “Right then,” I continue, “wait here till I get back.”

I dash off upstairs to Little Albert’s storeroom and return with a bucket of warm soapy water and a sponge.

“There you are,” I tell him, “get stuck into it.” I go round to the driver to ask him to inspect the work when the boy claims to have finished, as I shall have to put in an appearance in the playground. When I get back to the rear-end, Tony is standing with his arms folded in what is obviously a gesture of defiance.

“Like that is it?” I say grimly. “Right, matey – I’ll give you just ten seconds. If you haven’t started by then, I shall dip *you* in the bucket and use you instead of the sponge.”

He takes about half that time to make up his mind, which is the better alternative. Picking up the sponge as if it’s likely to go off in his hand, he starts dabbing at he metal.

“For crying out loud!” I roar at him, “you’re supposed to be washing the thing not powdering its bottom.” I snatch the sponge from him, dunk it in the water and with an artistic flourish, saturate a large area, himself included. “Like that,” I tell him. “Now get on with it. I’ve got better things to do than stand here watching you prancing about. When you’ve finished, wash the sponge and bucket out, wring out the sponge and leave them outside my door. Have you got all that?”

9:30 am. The tide of bodies flooding out of the playground towards the warmth of the school tells me that it’s too late to go up there and inspect the troops, so I go straight up to the classroom. Grins of malicious anticipation from the boys greet me and I soon see why. Andrew Miller is favouring us with one of his rare appearances. He never was noted for regular attendance lower down the school and now that he is a Leaver he hardly shows up at all. This is a blessing anyway, because there is always bother whenever he does take the trouble to visit us.

“Well, look what the bin-men left behind,” I greet him cordially. “What’s matter this time – couldn’t you sleep?” He just gives me his big daft dog grin by way of a reply. He is quite an easy lad to get on with really and has fair potential but I can’t see him ever making anything of his life. He thrives on getting into trouble and already has a considerable police record for petty offences. He is the despair of his mother, poor soul, and the delight of his father, of whom he is the image in every respect.

"What are you going to do about Carol Crawford?" This query distracts me from investigating the mystery of the Miller reappearance. It comes from the girls' side of the room and I look across to see four of them, arms folded across their bosoms, heads on one side, lips pressed righteously together – like a row of juvenile Les Dawsons. I can see them all in ten years' time – curlers, slippers, and no teeth.

"What about Carol Crawford?" I ask innocently though I know what they are getting at. We go to the Sports Centre in town on Tuesday mornings. There, everybody has more or less a free choice of activity, under specialist instruction. The boys love it, but for some reason the girls seem to look on it as an ordeal. For several weeks now, Carol has taken to arriving late every Tuesday morning – so late in fact that we have had to set off without her. On arriving back at school, the girls have found to their chagrin that she has spent the morning doing cosy little jobs for various members of staff. The seething resentment has built up over the weeks against her, and I am being cast in the role of villain because of my apparent lack of action in the matter. It looks as if the situation is going to be aggravated this morning as there is no sign of her yet again.

"All right, if she doesn't turn up in time this morning I really will do something about it." I have the feeling that I must have said that before, a notion borne out by the outbursts that follow.

"You always say that."

"You never do anything about it."

"She just does what she wants."

"What *are* you going to do about it then?"

The shafts all strike home with a force that makes me wince. "All right, all right. It's not as easy as all that and there isn't much I *can* do when she's not here. She might be poorly for all we know or she might have had an accident on the way to school."

"Huh!"

"You want to make 'er 'ave 'er dinner wi' t'littluns."

"Take 'er bus-pass off 'er."

These and other helpful suggestions pour in until I angrily call a halt. "Come on now wrap it up. It's time we were on our way or we shall all be late. Get your things together and look sharp."

9:45 am. We set off to walk the three-quarters of a mile or so to the sports centre, down the drive, through Bridge Street and then along the main road. They always complain about having to walk when we could go in the minibus but I tell them that it's good for them. Actually it would be easier if we did ride as they get plenty of exercise at the sports centre, so the walk is really for my benefit. It is, in fact, a strain on the nerves walking informally along the busy road for obvious reasons. I don't like to treat them like babies by keeping them all together holding hands as it were, so we all make our own way there at our own pace. The keen ones forge ahead but the less energetic dawdle along. The price I have to pay for my slice of the exercise is to jump neurotically every time I hear a horn or a squeal of brakes.

I am enjoying the stroll along Bridge Street, a tranquil Victorian avenue which serves as a short cut between the school grounds and the main road, when I hear footsteps rapidly catching up with me from the rear. Out of the corner of my eye, I see that I have been joined by someone intent on destroying my meditations.

"Good morning, Thir." It is a huge smile accompanied by its owner, Imtiaz.

"Good morning to you too, Imtiaz, and are you well?"

"Oh yeth, Thir, thank you, Thir! My better ith back."

Ah, here we go! It's time for 'spot the saying'. Now Imtiaz is the unwitting master of every grammatical and syntactic distortion of the English language known to man. Every week he falls in step with me and tests my skill at deciphering his latest phrase or saying. It's great fun! I see it as a kind of simulated television panel game. An imaginary quizmaster in my head keeps up the usual patter – "Right viewers! Our resident panellist, Ben Bailey, once more has until the end of Bridge Street to unravel this week's poser set by that master of the insoluble – Imtiaz Ahmed Ali! And—this week's saying is—'My better is back'."

Of course, Imtiaz is not privy to all this excitement and atmosphere at all – he just thinks I have gone temporarily barmy! A slightly perplexed smile replaces the customary broad one as I frantically rack my brain to unscramble the message.

Ah – got it in one this time! "'My brother is back'. Your brother, who went to Pakistan for a holiday, has come back. That's it isn't it eh, Imtiaz?" I declare confidently.

"No, Thir."

Er – now – let me see. "Got it now Imtiaz – 'My brother is black'."

"No, Thir." The smile becomes slightly more puzzled. Well I suppose it was a bit of a feeble attempt.

"My brother is better?" Shake of the head. Let's get off the brother theme for a while. "My butter is bad?" Still no joy. By now things are getting desperate and we are down to the last few yards of the street. The invisible quizmaster is still pounding away in my head – "Only another twenty yards to go and Imtiaz will once again be the winner!"

Got it! Of course – how could I have been to dim – "'My brother is bad!' That's it isn't it, Imtiaz?" I almost beg him. "You know, you're always telling me how your brother bullies you aren't you?"

"No, Thir. Brother isth thtill in Pakithtan." Imtiaz is clearly once more totally bewildered by the colossal stupidity of his teacher. It's all perfectly obvious to him, but dumbo in charge seems incapable of grasping even the simplest bit of information.

Gong! Time! "And Imtiaz wins again! That puts him ahead by three to one in this term's series," crows the quizmaster as we turn out of Bridge Street, along the side of the canal for a few yards before joining the main road.

"All right, Imtiaz – I give in. I can't get this one at all. Give me it again or see if someone else can twig it."

"Martin Thitonth, Martin Thithonth, come here," he calls to Martin Sissons, his bosom-pal. "I am telling Thir that my better ith back but he doeth not know what I am thaying to him."

"Well," I challenge 'Scissors' rather crossly, "what is he on about then?"

"He means his back is better, Sir," explains Martin incredulously. "Don't you remember he had to miss PE 'cos he had a bad back?"

Well the crafty snake! He's hit me with a sneaky inversion when I was looking for something more complicated altogether. I had even thought of going for a spoonerism!

I take defeat badly on this occasion, trudging morosely along the pavement, all alone. I am not even consoled by the warmth of the sun on this glorious, spirit-lifting day. I am joking of course.

10:00 am. We arrive at the sports centre and I just make myself useful seeing to it that everyone is in the right place with the right equipment.

A mixed group go to judo, some of the girls have what is know as 'ladies' keep-fit'. Another mixed group play badminton. Finally, a small group goes to the swimming pool. I have to watch this last lot most carefully, as the attendants are not keen to take responsibility for pupils who are there on school time. There would of course be a terrible fuss if anyone were to drown or get involved in other serious trouble. Some parents are like that you know, unreasonable—.

I decide to spend the first part of the session with the judo enthusiasts. It turns out to be a wise choice, as the instructor has not yet arrived. She has them well drilled insomuch as they know where to find the uniforms, but one or two of them have difficulty putting them on, particularly the belt, which requires a complicated knot.

Alvin is usually the most ham-fisted, so I give him a hand and between us we soon have him looking very martial. I'm not too sure that he's all that keen on judo actually, but it does give him a legitimate excuse to get his hands on the brawny Maria, for whom he is currently carrying a torch. From what little I have seen, however, he doesn't seem to have many opportunities of doing that, as she is exceptionally skilful and throws him around like a packet of crisps. At the moment though, he appears to have other things on his mind. With Alvin it is never a case of 'ignore it and it will go away', so I had better make some enquiries.

"You all right, Alvin?"

"No, Sir."

"What's the matter then – don't you feel well?"

When Alvin is confused or embarrassed, he twists his head round and rocks the upper part of his body backwards and forwards. I notice this happening now so obviously something is amiss.

"Come on, Alvin – what *is* wrong?"

More writhing and wriggling follow at an increased tempo so I judge that we are on the verge of discovery.

"I can't get me cock out, Sir," he eventually explains.

"I didn't realise that you needed it out to do judo," I reply, confused.

"No, Sir," he bursts out with a huge guffaw, then noticing that everyone has turned to see what is so funny, lowers his voice and completes the explanation – "I got to go to the lav."

This time it's my turn to roar with laughter, which causes a resumption of attention on us and the return of Alvin's discomposure. "Why didn't you go before you got all your gear on then?" I hiss at him.

"I din't want to go then," he hisses back at me.

The problem is really down to the fact that Alvin can't tie or untie the simplest knot, let alone this one, which regulates the all-important judo belt. After a good deal of tugging and pulling, we manage to release him so that he can dash down the corridor for a little light relief. Whilst he is away, the instructor arrives so I am happy to leave the return half of the problem in her capable hands (as it were!).

I realise that this unexpected interruption has delayed my visit to the swimmers. I usually give them a few minutes to get changed so that I am not hanging about wasting time, but by now they will surely be in the water. I have visions of bloating bodies lying on the bottom of the pool and this spurs me into a dash along the passage to the 'wet-side' of the building.

To my relief, all is peaceful when I arrive. I know the attendant who gives me a thumbs-up signal, meaning that I can safely leave them to get on with whatever they want to do within reason and he will keep an eye on them.

That only leaves the racket players in the main hall, and that completes the first tour of inspection. There is no hurry to reach them, as their instructor is always right on the ball or shuttle whichever is the case, so I can recover my breath as I make my way at a more leisurely pace back to the ‘dry-side’.

I peep through the door of the judo room en route, and see that all is well. Bodies are hurtling through the air and heads thudding against the floor with great regularity so I can leave them in peace (a euphemism in this case of course).

In the main hall, the badminton instructor is supervising a game with the air of someone who has just received a telegram containing news of a bereavement. I join him. The game is between Pixie and Dixie, but is more like ballet. They float around the court in slow motion, making badminton-like gestures with the rackets but never actually making contact with the shuttle.

The action appears to have a hypnotic effect on the instructor. He stands there, mouth ajar, eyes glazed.

Eventually he breaks the silence, but his expression remains fixed.

“It’s been weeks now and I don’t think they’ve hit the bloody thing twice in all that time. I can’t understand it – twenty years and I’ve never been beaten like this before.”

“Well – I don’t think they’ve ever been so far apart before,” I try to comfort him. “Perhaps they would be better holding the same racket and having someone else at the other side of the net.” I feel that a little joke might help to restore his balance.

“Do you have them every day?” he asks, ignoring my flippancy.

“Part of every day – yes.”

“God Almighty!” he murmurs reverently.

I look round uneasily, noticing the absence of Peter, Arthur, Jeremy and Andrew. I query this with the instructor.

“They seemed to be getting a bit bored with badminton so I sent them up to the squash courts. They’ve played a bit before so I thought they’d be OK on their own. I’ll go up and check them out if you don’t mind staying here with these two.”

The prospect of being lumbered with Pixie and Dixie for the rest of the session holds little appeal, so with an affectation of great self-sacrifice I insist that it will be no trouble at all to go and look in on the rest of the gang now that I have come so far.

The squash courts are up a steep flight of stairs. The gradient forces me to slow down, which in turn enables me to hear the noise around me, or rather the lack of it. In fact, the unnatural quiet disturbs me. I don't like uproar, but silence is unnerving.

First impressions are often deceptive and this proves to be no exception. Startled looks are the usual greeting, but incredibly everything is calm.

I seem to have hit on rest period. Big Arthur and Peter Howard are on court, but having a breather. Up here in the gallery, Jeremy Knight is using his racket as an imaginary guitar, crooning discordantly as he strums his fingers across the strings. Andrew Miller is sitting with his back to me, gazing down at the court.

Arthur and Peter grin up at me, in anticipation it seems to me, Jeremy sees me but just rolls his eyes and continues his dirge as I ask, "Why aren't you all playing when there are spare courts?"

My voice has an electrifying effect on Andrew Miller though. Obviously unaware of my arrival until now, he leaps to his feet and turns to face me but not before I catch a glimpse of something whirling from his grasp into the court below.

"Put your foot on it! Put your foot on it!" he grates out of the corner of his mouth to the two below.

Thinking that perhaps it's a 'mucky picture' or a note, I casually glance over the guard rail. Neither of the resting players has put his foot on 'it', and 'it' is glowing cheerfully on the expensive floor of the course.

"Put your foot on it before it damages the floor." This time I give the order and Peter grinds the smouldering butt to death, leaving an ugly black smear on the grain-coloured boards. I turn furiously on Miller. "You are nothing but a damn nuisance. You show your face once a blue moon and when you do there's always trouble."

He mutters something about needing a fag and I tear into him again – "Need a fag! *Need* a fag! How old are you?"

"Fifteen."

"Fifteen years old and you *need* a fag. Before long you'll find you're *needing* a bottle, then you'll be *needing* a hypodermic. Next thing you'll be sleeping under newspapers on a park bench." I pause for breath and the daft dog grin creeps over his face again as he sees his mates having hysterics below. This only rekindles my anger. "Look lad. I'm simply not prepared to leave you where you can't be seen. Get yourself changed and go and sit in the main foyer where you are in full view all the time."

"Where's that?"

"By the kiosk where they take the money."

"What's a kiosk?"

"Don't push your luck!"

Sensing the possibility of imminent GBH, he mooches sullenly down to the changing room and I turn back to the court. "Find something to clean up that floor with please," I ask Arthur and David. "How long do you intend sitting there like a redundant Rolling Stone?" I ask Jeremy Knight sharply.

"We're taking it in turns to play so we don't get too tired," is the explanation.

"That *would* be a tragedy wouldn't it – you wearing yourself out," I scoff. "Let's face it, you need a week in bed to recover from combing your hair." He just treats me to his sickly grin by way of an answer this time.

10:45 am. I hurry off to check the progress of the others dotted about the building. The swimmers have already left the pool so I can rest easy. The judo-ists are having their final free-for-all, so Alvin might just get lucky after all. Pixie and Dixie are reaching the climax of their shuttle-less ballet, watched still by the, now, apparently comatose instructor, and the keep-fit girls are writhing on the floor, which means presumably that they are doing an exercise or they have been machine-gunned by their leader.

I decide to have a last look at the squash players before calling a halt. As I pass through the foyer I see Andrew Miller sitting gloomily on a bench tapping his fingers together between his knees. He looks up as he sees me but I just give him a withering glare.

To my amazement, Jeremy is on court when I reach the top of the stairs. Big Arthur is sitting out this time but Peter is obviously finding his new opponent's girlish efforts to make contact with the little ball so hilarious that he spends most of his time collapsing on the floor shrieking with laughter. In consequence, a genuine contest is out of the question.

11:00 am. This seems to be a good time to finish, so I send the squash players off to the changing room and gradually retrace my steps until all have been accounted for.

As a rule, everyone changes at their leisure and we all finish up in the snack bar upstairs. Those who want or can afford, have a little *light* refreshment then we all make our separate ways back to school.

Today must have been especially hectic in the judo room as the boys decide to have a shower. This causes some delay because it means that I have to hang back until the last one is dried and clothed to make sure that no accidents occur.

By the time I arrive upstairs, they have all been served. I am pleased to see that they have stuck to the request to keep it to a minimum – all except one, that is. Typically, Jeremy Knight has in front of him two pork pies, chips, beans, a piece of apple tart, a Mars Bar and a milkshake.

"You get right up my nose," I inform him without preamble.

"What's up?" he asks in his usual tone of injured innocence.

"Only that I've asked you a dozen times or more to have no more than a drink and a biscuit in here because it will soon be lunch-time at school. *Then*, your plate will be piled so high with food that you'll have to stand up to see over the top of it. *Then*, you'll proceed to waste more than half of it as usual because you will *already* have stuffed yourself full of food."

"I pay for it," he asserts indignantly. "Anyway I can't help it if I'm starving."

"For a start you do *not* pay for it – your mother, God help her, does," I snap back at him, "and secondly you are *not* starving, you are just showing off. You are a GREEDY… OBNOXIOUS… TOAD! What are you?"

"A greedy, ozb—"

"Obnoxious."

"Ob – noxious – toad," he finally splutters out accompanied by his slimy grin, evidently delighted with his new status, especially as Arthur and Peter are having fits of glee at the other side of the table.

"Where's Miller?" I cut in, suddenly aware of a significant gap in the ranks.

"In the lav," Peter informs me conscientiously, and adds, "nudge nudge, wink wink, say no more, know what I mean?"

Without a word I get up and walk through to the toilets. A quick glance around is enough to tell that the room is empty apart from Andrew Miller, harmlessly washing his hands in one of the bowls.

Relieved at being spared another confrontation with him, I am just about to withdraw when, out of the corner of my eye, almost under my nose in fact, I see a faint glow. Closer inspection shows it to be a lighted cigarette perched on the formica ledge, obviously awaiting the next puff from its owner. I look from the boy to the cigarette and back again.

"I just do not *believe* this," I say in amazement.

"It's not mine," he counters hurriedly, looking round as if searching for the real owner.

"I suppose it belongs to the fellow who went out as I came in," I say scathingly.

"Yeah, that's it. He must have left it when he went out."

"You PRAT! There wasn't anybody coming out as I came in and there has not been anybody in or out of here for the last five minutes. You know as well as I do who that tab belongs to."

He looks down and scuffs the ground with his toe as I go on – "Next week you can stay behind at school when the others come here. I don't see why I should waste my time wet-nursing you and leaving everybody else at risk while you're down here. Now get out of my sight – at the moment you're a complete nuisance. If you only realised it you could have quite a bit going for you, but only if you're prepared to make the effort."

Once more he drags his feet and slouches away from me in disgrace. I wonder as I watch his back if what I say will ever have any effect on him.

11:30 am. A rather subdued party trails in small groups back to school. At the top of the drive I glance across to the main buildings and see Marion Firth, our secretary, waving frantically to me and cupping her hand to her ear – I am wanted on the telephone.

I dash across and gasp my thanks as I take the receiver from her.

"Hello – is that Mr Bailey?" asks a voice in a broad Welsh accent.

Great! I recognise the voice, but resisting the temptation to say 'allo lovely boy', I restrict myself to a guarded – "Speaking".

"Griffiths yer from Nether Royd School. Nice to yer from yew again," he continues. I was wondrin' if we could perhaps arrange a football match – you know like the cricket we had last term. Do you remember?"

Do I remember? Do I ever! Trying to keep the malicious glee out of my voice, I wink across the table at Marion who smiles innocent encouragement at me. Without a tremor (I hope) I reply, "Yes, I think we could manage that. What day were you thinking of?"

"I suppose Friday this week would be a bit short notice eh?"

"Not at all, not at all. Friday will be perfect. What time can we expect you?"

"We'll come ready changed 'cos your facilities are a bit rough from what I can remember. Two o'clock suit yew?"

I compose myself with an effort after that last crack and say, with as much civility as I can manage in the circumstances, "two o'clock will be fine. We'll look forward to that. See you Friday then."

Not much we won't! In case you are wondering why an adult should be indulging in such apparently small-minded scheming, suffice it to say that none of us likes to be conned.

I like to think that I am nobody's fool, but the cricket match last term to which my learned friend (who is the Head of the school incidentally) has just referred, was the biggest con of my life, and I fell into it like a great dumb animal! I wouldn't say that he actually *cheated*, but every trick in the book was used and I fell for the lot.

You could put it down to complacency on my part. We had such a good side that there was virtually no way that we could lose, but having said that I wanted to make sure that our opponents were not humiliated. I intended, with a little manipulation, that we should finish up with the appearance of a close contest, as we often have to do in special school games.

What I hadn't reckoned on was an opponent who intended to *win* – full-stop! I have lived since then with my own shame at being so blatantly gulled, coupled with the spectre of my players' contempt for me on this occasion for letting them down so badly.

Now at last comes the chance to redress the balance!

12:00 noon. A quick check to make sure that all is well in the 'Mansion' passing my hungry charges on the way across to lunch. Everything is fine, so with the thought of Friday's game fresh in my mind, I will go out and have a look at the field.

Tuesday is middle school games afternoon, so the inspection will kill two birds with one stone. As I said before, the whole school stands on clay so as the first of the winter rains arrive, the ground becomes a mire from which it never recovers until it dries out like concrete in the blistering heat of the Yorkshire summer!

The first few steps onto the turf bring water oozing over the tops of my shoes and this is the best bit! A glance ahead confirms the worst. Miniature lakes dot the whole area as far as the opposite goal line, so I shall have to give some serious thought as to its fitness.

12:15 pm. In to lunch, exchanging pleasantries with the seven dwarfs who are engaged in a pitched battle with cheese flan. That's good – I love cheese flan. I always maintain that no better dish was ever served in a first-class restaurant than our cook's cheese flan.

Obviously something is going on at the table where I sit down to eat. Big Arthur, Peter, Jeremy and Andrew are all exchanging foolish grins and occasionally erupting into laughter, directing their looks as me as they do so. Perhaps there is something comical about my appearance, but their silliness irritates me, particularly after the events of the morning, so rather than be an old misery, I eat up quickly and leave.

12:30 pm. Across to the 'Mansion' to relieve Mary for the rest of the session. I make a start by kicking out half a dozen of her lot who are racing each other up and down the stairs. My own folk are strangely quiet so I don't tempt providence by disturbing them, and decide that it may be a good time to catch up on a few admin chores.

I swear that there must be a switch in my behind which comes into operation every time I sit down, and sure enough, before I can reach my pen, there is a knock on the door. Standing outside is a stern-faced Elsie Davidson, one of our NTAs, clutching by the hand a small tearful boy.

The boy is Thomas McDougall, the younger of the McDougall brothers, the one I call 'Young McDougall' because I can never quite remember which one is which. These two are always in trouble, mainly through mischief rather than malice, so naturally I fix him with an icy glare.

"Well?" I demand. He looks down at the floor and if I didn't know him better, I would swear that he is crying. This would be most unusual as the brothers McDougall are as tough as a pair of old boots.

"Mr Bailey, I'd like you to have a look at this if you will," says Elsie, tilting Tommy's head upwards to expose his whole face.

"Good heavens!" I exclaim as I see the state of his right cheekbone. "Now how the blazes did this happen?" His cheek is sporting a still-swelling red lump with an ugly purple and white core.

The lad looks down again, biting his trembling lip. I usher them into my office and sit them both down whilst Elsie takes up the story.

"Him," she says pointing to Tommy, "and Clifford Talman were up the fire escape by the domestic science room, where they shouldn't be of course," she hints in a slightly louder voice, "when he suddenly let out such a yell and they both came flying down the steps. Then I see the state of his face."

"Now then – er – Young McDougall, think very carefully," I say, taking up the story, "have you any idea how this happened?"

He shakes his head slowly. Not a word out of him so far.

"Did you and Clifford have a fight?" Again he shakes his head so I am forced to persist. "What did you feel then?"

At last he comes to life and tells me in a small, quavering voice, "Sir, there was just this bang on me face and me and Clifford ran back down t'ladder."

"What were you doing when you felt this bang?"

"We was just looking through that big window." Presumably he means the fire escape doors.

"Was the window open?"

"No, Sir."

"And nobody opened it while you were up there?"

"No, Sir."

"The window isn't broken now is it?"

"No, Sir."

"Did you hear anything at all?"

Before he can reply, Elsie cuts in to relieve the monotony of his answers – "You know what the noise is like in the playground. You can't hear yourself speak."

"I don't suppose you saw anything lying on the floor – a stone or anything like that?"

"No, Sir," he resumes the litany.

I manoeuvre my body around, simulating in my imagination the boys' positions outside the window as a thought, prompted by the neat contours of the swelling, now puffing out under his eye, strikes me.

"Would you like to take him across to Nurse, Mrs Davidson, whilst I have a little stroll round the playground?" Turning to Tommy I say, lest we forget, "You'll think twice about going up those stairs again won't you?"

"Yes, Sir" he replies, varying his pattern slightly as he groggily follows Elsie across the yard.

I tag along behind but only as far as the bottom of the stairs, from where I turn in the opposite direction, through the fire doors, first checking for signs of Savage Beast, and into the playground.

Where to begin? That is the question. I study the playground and its occupants. There is a game of football at each end, a couple of girls' skipping groups, boys climbing trees and the usual scrimmage of kids doing nothing in particular other than chase each other round and round, letting out deafening noises.

What am I hoping for is a piece of luck. I think I know what I'm looking for, but the key to it lies in coming across one of our regular informers who might just have seen something interesting happen. Every school has its quota of these characters. They simply want attention and passing on their tit-bits of information guarantees them at least a little.

I mingle with the throng, wearing what I fondly imagine to be a benevolent, encouraging look. It's like fishing in a way – it attracts one or two minnows at first, youngsters who come up and walk a few paces holding your hand, but it's the bigger fish we want though, and they are not so easily tempted.

However, today is one of those lucky days. Before long, a much more useful specimen slithers alongside in the shape of Timothy Jay. The fishing image is most appropriate in his case, as he is built something like an eel with legs. He is one of those unfortunate boys who never have an established circle of friends nor even a regular single fellow-sufferer. He is, without wishing to be unkind, the lowest form of playground life. He wriggles from the fringes of one group to another, tolerated or suffered for a while, depending on how much malicious amusement can be wrung out of him. He is then usually rejected with jeers and kicks or punches to retire, whimpering to the sanctuary of the duty-teacher.

"'Lo, Sir."

"Hello, Timothy – all right are we today?" I enquire encouragingly.

"Yes, Sir." There follows a short pause as he arranges his next few words into the correct order. "Sir, Warren's got a gun."

"A GUN!" Although my suspicions are in the process of being confirmed the words 'a gun' conjure up visions of a Beretta or a twelve-bore, not the expected catapult or air-pistol. Hence the over-reaction. I try to retrieve the situation by lowering my voice, at the same time glancing around to make sure that no interest has been aroused.

"How do you know he's got a gun?" I ask.

"There was a lot of 'em all shootin' it and they wouldn't let me have a go." This is obviously a case of 'if you can't join 'em, beat 'em'.

"When did it happen?"

"This mornin' before we went into school then a bit since."

"How long since?"

"Just now."

Knowing our pupils' sense of time, 'just now' will probably fit the bill as far as Tommy's injury is concerned. I look round for Warren and see him standing in on the football match at the far end of the playground. I use the words 'standing in', advisedly in Warren's case because although I often see him in the middle of a game, with his satellites, I don't recall ever having seen him actually make contact with the ball unless it has hit him by pure mischance.

'Popular' is not the adjective that one would use to describe Warren. Nevertheless he is always the centre of a sizeable following, attracted, in all fairness more by his 'novelty value' than by his charisma. In fact, he is a horror as far as the staff are concerned. His bland, moon-like face, topped by a puff of dandelion hair, never registers any emotion, whatever the situation. He is invariably at the centre of any disturbance in his class, but nailing him as the culprit is almost an impossibility. His ability to parry, deflect, and flatly deny, often causes his accusers to doubt what they have witnessed with their own eyes.

My opinion is that, like so many of his type, the trouble begins at home. Who was it that said 'the worst people in the world to have children are parents'? Warren's father, it is said by those who know the family, claims that he is determined to 'make a man of him'. Well, if dragging the lad round the pubs and clubs, getting him plastered at the age of fourteen, and furnishing him with an endless supply of expensive playthings, is going to do that, then he has not much further to go. Add to all that the encouragement to believe in his own infallibility and you have an ego that will never sag – and that is Warren.

I stand for a while, wondering about the best way to tackle the problem, and decide that there will be no point in quizzing Warren. Accusation and confrontation are the only means – and then it's a slim chance – of catching him off guard. There is also a back-up policy, which forms in my mind if the first one fails, so I turn again to Timothy – "You said there were a lot of them with the gun this morning. Can you remember who they were?"

He screws up his face as an aid to concentration and says, "Warren, Charles, Delroy, Patrick—" His voice gradually tails off as he reaches the last name and I know that anyone named after that is simply on his own personal 'hit-list'. In any case there are enough big names to be going on with – three hard cases and one softy. The last named, Patrick Flynn, tags along with the tough-guys even though he is as soft as a boiled turnip. Even so, he wouldn't dare open his mouth against the others.

Let's go then – as they say in the movies. First I move in and shepherd Warren to the side of the pitch. "You're in dead trouble mate. The shot you fired at that lad this morning has hit him right under his eye. Nurse says he could lose his eye, so you had better come across with that gun of yours before there's any more damage and it's a matter for the police."

If I thought that such shock tactics would panic him into an instant breakdown, then I have sadly under-estimated him. So far, his eyes have been fixed beyond me, watching the progress of the game. Now he swivels them round squarely onto my face and says, "I 'ampt gorrer gun. I don't know anything about it," and adds as he sees me looking at the pile of coats and bags piled up as goalposts, "you can search me if you want."

A straight bat! What else could I expect? If he could play cricket like that he would go on to play for England.

I know that there is not the faintest hope, in view of Warren's invitation to have an inspection; nevertheless I call the players together to the middle of the pitch. A quick glance round shows that nobody has anything like a gun concealed on his person, as they are all stripped down to the minimum for their game, so I ask them all to collect their gear and empty it on the ground for examination.

As usual, when you are looking eagerly for something, you rarely find what you want, but find instead something for which you have previously searched. This time proves to be no exception. The weapon, of course, fails to show up but I collect a couple of packets of cigarettes, a box of matches, two pornographic magazines and a pack of lewd playing cards. The unexpected nature of the raid has taken the unwary by surprise, but the ones who matter are obviously prepared.

Disappointed but not surprised, I call the four main suspects down to my office. There are vehement protests, but I brush them aside.

"Right then," I begin with the air of one who has all the facts. "Let's not waste any more time. As you know, a boy has been hit near the eye by an object and is in a very serious condition. Now let's have the truth before it's too late and we have to call the law in."

The last little broadside fails to unnerve even Patrick Flynn, so they have obviously decided to see this through together to the death.

“I ’ampt got no gun,” snarls Delroy, lip curling in his usual offensive expression.

“I don’t know nothing about no gun,” says Charles with unaccustomed mildness.

“I don’t know nothing,” echoes Patrick, obviously terrified of saying the wrong thing, as the others turn in a body and fix him with an intimidating glare.

“Who said anything about a gun?” I ask almost casually, “all I said was someone had been hit by an object. It could have been thrown or catapulted – I never said it had been fired from a gun.”

“We don’t know *nothing*,” says Warren with great finality.

1:15 pm. “Fair enough then,” I continue, realising that it’s time I was getting ready for the afternoon session, “I’ll want you all in Mr Coburn’s office after school or else—”

“But we’ll miss the buses,” they chorus.

“Hard luck – but not one of you leaves before this business is cleared up. Now get yourselves back into the yard until the whistle blows.”

1:35 pm. I am late getting to the gym for games, as I expected I would be. The result is that the class, having had to wait ten minutes, is milling around outside like scalded ants. The reason for my late arrival is that I have been to see Nurse to ask her to take Young McDougall home so he can’t be seen and got at. Then I went to see Clive Coburn to ask if he will join me on the bench at the after-school court, to which he readily agreed. It is amazing how much more can be achieved by two rather than one in such matters of stalemate.

A bellow of rage from me sends them scurrying back into line. They are a fairly docile bunch apart from one or two tearaways, so we usually have an enjoyable afternoon.

However, it does them no harm to be squashed now and again so I start with a rucking about the line-up. “I don’t know how many times I have to tell you to get in line when you come down to games. One of these days I shall make you spend the whole session practising just standing quietly in line. You’ll enjoy that when there’s snow on the ground won’t you?”

“No, Sir,” call out twenty-four voices fervently, followed by the statutory mass-shiver at the thought. They will have forgotten by next week, but it brings them to heel for the moment.

"All right then – WALK into the changing-room and sit down. DON'T get changed yet because I have a few words to say."

They file in and sit in silence. "I've been out on the field and it's like a swamp," I begin, but groans from the enthusiasts interrupt me and, at the same time, drown the sighs of relief from the faint-hearted – "BUT, what I have decided is that we will spend the first half of the session in the gym up to break, then after break you can put your outdoor gear on and we'll go out on the field." I pause as the news receives a mixed greeting. "So now get changed – we've wasted enough time."

Whilst they get ready, six figures stand up, walk to the end of the room where I am and stand there sheepishly.

"Well?" I ask them, as if I didn't know.

"We 'ampt gorrus things," their spokesman informs me.

There are four regular skivers, including the spokesman, plus Old McDougall and another poor ragged little lad called Peter Johnson. The last two, I know, come from real breadline families and sports gear is the last thing on their shopping list.

As it happens, the PTA has recently made us a donation of several pairs of shorts. These I intend to loan to deserving cases and this seems a good place to start.

"You four stand over here," I tell the skivers, pointing with my left hand, "you two over here," indicating the other side. "Now then Old McDougall – how are things on that farm?" His face goes through a range of expressions but he says nothing as I go on. "Let me see now – how does the next verse go – Old McDougall had a farm eeyi eeyio, and on that farm they had no shorts—is that right so far?"

He lets his face slip into the slightest of grins and mutters, "Yes, Sir."

"What about you Peter – still no shorts?"

He shakes his head, almost in tears, so to spare them further humiliation, I quickly hand them each a pair of shorts out of the storeroom.

"Now these are for you to look after – to take home, to wash, to bring to school for PE and games, to love and to cherish, to have and to hold, from this day forward, till the end of term when you will hand them back to me or I'll chop your ears off –

understand? Now go and get changed."

They skip joyously off into the changing room. I feel that this is a far better way of doing things (if it works) than the embarrassment, for them, of a weekly handout.

Turning to the other four I explain my apparent discrimination to them – "You probably think it's unfair that I should give to them and not to you. *But*, without going into details, there are good reasons why they have no kit. You, on the other hand, have got kit and I'm not prepared to chase around after people who are too idle or forgetful to bother. If I do that, nobody will ever make an effort to bring their stuff. Whilst we're at it, what's your excuse?" I ask the first lad.

"Forgorrem, Sir," he replies as I tut and look skywards.

"You?" I ask the second.

"I forgorrem an' all, Sir," to the accompaniment of a snort of derision from me.

"Mine's still in 't drier. Me mam forgot ter tek 'em out," is the third excuse.

"Your mam would have been better sending your shorts and putting you in the drier," I tell him witheringly.

"Can I do it in me trousers?" ask the fourth.

"Can you what?!" I ask bewildered.

"Can I play games in me trousers?" he persists.

"It all depends what kind of games you have in mind," I reply cautiously.

"Can I play with the others in me trousers," he tries once more.

"I think I know what you mean by now – and the answer is no, you can't do it in your trousers, as you put it. If you can't be bothered to bring your things then you deserve to sit out."

"But me shorts 'ave gorrole in 'em and me mam 'ant 'ad time to mend it," he pleads.

"Has your mam had time to go to bingo?" I counter.

"Yes, Sir," he replies.

"Then she's had time to fix your shorts, so go home and blame her and not me. Anyway that's it as far as I'm concerned." I live in hope that some day one of these parents will turn up and challenge me on comments like this, but there has been no such luck so far. It would be really gratifying to show some of them just how hard they can make life for their kids at such times. The trouble is that some of the parents don't know it's Tuesday till Friday – then we wonder why so many of our youngsters are slow. To be completely fair all-round though, it is just possible that sometimes parents are not reminded when it is PE or games day and it is reasonable to expect that, presumably, they do have other things to carry round in their heads. I'm tempted to add to the last remark, but I think maybe that's enough for now.

The four of them are still hanging about, so I shall have to find them something discouraging to do. "OK you lot – up to the wallbars and sit on the top one." They groan, but I am determined that they are not just going to have a soft option, so I watch until they are all installed on the topmost perch where, after half an hour or so, sitting on the narrow bar becomes excruciatingly painful and the resolve forms (hopefully) never again to come without kit.

Meanwhile, the lads have come into the gym in ones and twos and are raring to go.

"Right – let's have you all lined up against the far wall and we'll have some races to warm you up."

"Aw, Sir! Why can't we play five-a-side?" complains one of the football stars.

"We'll play five-a-side later. Just remember that not everybody likes to play football all the time."

We have some hectic individual relay races, which leave them all gasping. We follow that up by joining all the races together, which totally prostrates them. The winners are invariably from the same small group, but there is fierce competition right down the list. At the very end, Peter Richardson, an enormous fat lad who gets about only with extreme difficulty, always has a titanic struggle not to lose out to wee Ian Noakes who has severe cerebral palsy, which cruelly affects his mobility.

I goad them back to their feet only to tell them 'mat rugby' which brings more groans of dismay from the purists but beams of joy from those who are built more for comfort than for speed. The reason is that, in this game, the big clumsy lads have a chance to shine, as the object of it is to gain possession of a medicine ball and somehow propel it along, either by passing it or carrying it, until it can be touched down on the opponents' mat –

much as a try is scored in real rugby. In this game, therefore, it is an advantage to be as big as possible for obvious reasons.

I always pick the teams whatever game we play. At first, I used to let them pick their own, but experience taught me that of course all the best players finished up on the same side and nobody else ever had a look in. So, for mat rugby I make sure that each team has its fair share of 'fatties'.

The game is really an amorphous shambles. For a start, it is almost impossible to pass a medicine ball any distance under pressure, so the obvious thing is to carry it.

With one mass of bodies pushing the player with the ball one way, against another mass of bodies pushing in the opposite direction, progress in the game is strictly limited. The best of three is, therefore, generally sufficient.

The result of this particular game is a personal triumph for Peter Richardson who is the actual ball carrier, making two successive touchdowns for his team under a mountain of players from both sides, after being torn this way and that for fully five minutes. This is about the maximum period that the human body can tolerate mat rugby.

As usual after such a game, the gym looks like a butcher's shop. The floor is spattered with droplets of blood and littered with aching bodies. People are gingerly examining a variety of cuts and bruises, but Peter outshines them all. The state of his face and his huge wobbling bulk is awesome. His trunk is a kaleidoscopic mural of wheals and scratches and his face looks as if it has been used to sweep the yard, but he is ecstatic. He positively basks in the united 'cor!'s' and 'wow!'s' and the pointing fingers as everyone's gaze is drawn to him. He scorns the idea that any of it hurts and refuses to attempt even the most minor repairs to his ravaged frame. He intends to enjoy every single moment in the spotlight. He knows that it will soon be midnight for him and he will be a pumpkin again until the next time.

With only a good twenty minutes of the session left, we shall have to move on to five-a-side football or it will seem an afternoon wasted for most of them. I hastily revise the teams to give as fair a balance as possible. Proper rules of football are observed but the team, which concedes a goal leaves the arena, the winners stay on and their next opponents arrive to do battle. The teams have to have themselves organised before they get on the pitch or they can be off again before they have even touched the ball. To be the winning team of course means that you have to spend more time on the pitch than anyone else. It doesn't need points, goals for or against, or league-tables for this – everyone knows instinctively who the winners are by the end.

The outcome of the games is usually quite predictable, though happily not to the players who always live in the hope of divine intervention. The truth is that in every group there is *one* star player and whatever side he is on is going to win, barring the unforeseen.

There is, however, one amusing diversion this afternoon. The wretched Timothy Jay is in this group and his misfortunes pursue him even onto the five-a-side pitch. He spends most of his time cowering away from the ball and wincing every time it comes near him. On this occasion, unfortunately for him, he is not agile enough to get out of the way of a well-struck ball, which smacks him right in the mouth. He goes down screaming and lies there moaning and twitching as everyone else falls about laughing insanely. After a while the game proceeds and, realising that nobody intends to go to his aid, he picks himself up groggily and totters feebly around for a few seconds. His highly-developed radar system must have been damaged by the first blow, however, as he never sees the next ball, struck even more firmly in the opposite direction. This time it scores a direct hit on his privates with a sickening explosion, sending him once more into death throes on the floor. The mass hysteria that this causes effectively brings the proceedings to an end, so wiping my eyes, I send them off to get changed and make an attempt to revive Timothy who, by this time, is coiled like a spring on the boards. If all this sounds a bit callous, I should point out that the ball that we use in the gym is only a football bladder covered with soft cloth, and would hardly be capable of tearing a hole in a wet toilet roll.

Still, we have afforded Peter his brief ascent to the pinnacle; the least we can do now is indulge Timothy in his hour of need. A few words of sympathy and encouragement persuade him that he might yet live, though the next twenty-four hours will be critical.

This is no mean feat, considering that everyone around is still convulsed at the recollection.

2:30 pm. Playtime, but everyone decides that a visit to the toilet is essential, so by the time I have ushered them all out of the changing room and got myself across to the staff room, the teapot is empty and I have to settle for a glass of water. Still, I get some malicious satisfaction from relating the Timothy's tale to the effect that none of them can finish the last of their tea for laughing.

2:40 pm. All back in the changing room to prepare to brave the elements. A quick kit inspection shows that few of them are adequately dressed for the job. There are some whose strip would not disgrace a World Cup star, but in spite of pleas to parents, others are still turning out in their best (and only) shoes, or even gym shoes in some cases. Some are warmly clad whilst others shiver in skimpy, holey, short-sleeved t-shirts.

Still, they all know what to expect and it isn't too cold, so we pick the two sides and hand out the identifying team bibs, which we do indoors to avoid having to stand around getting chilly.

This time I install the four non-combatants as corner flags and the game gets under way. Although I select the teams as evenly as I can, it is difficult to cater for every eventuality, and Reds score in the first few seconds before Blues have even decided who is going in goal. There are one or two protests but I ignore them. Blues then decide that, although I have made sure that each team has a competent goalkeeper, the mammoth Peter will occupy the position based on the facts that: a) he is too slow and cumbersome to be of any use upfield, and b) he occupies the largest area, therefore he should be hardest to beat.

Unhappily for Peter, midnight has arrived so to speak, as within a minute of taking up his duties between the posts, a long speculative shot trickles through the mud towards him. Grunting and groaning with the exertion, Peter spreads his legs wide and reaches down as far as he can get. In spite of his efforts, however, he is still inches short of the ball when it arrives. It continues its trickle under his hands, though his legs, and has just enough strength to crawl over the goal line and die.

Immediately he is surrounded by angry teammates all berating him, his pre-playtime triumphs instantly forgotten.

"Yer fat git!"

"Gerraht, jumbo! Thar useless!"

"Gie us that jersey – ah'm goin' in!"

To his credit though, Peter refuses to be intimidated. Pleased no doubt to be relieved of his duties, he throws down the keeper's jersey, points furiously at the sky and declares, "Aw shurrup you lot – you can't see a thing for that sun!" He then retires with as much majesty as his figure will allow, to the calmer pastures on the fringe of the action.

This is the stage at which refereeing in a special school becomes something of an acquired art. If you are not careful the losing team will abandon hope altogether and the result will be a landslide. As it is, whilst the Blues are still reeling from the last goal, they concede a third. This one is hammered in from a distance of about eighteen inches by Old McDougall, who leaps in the air and goes through a *Match Of The Day* routine – sinking to his knees and blowing kisses to the terraces.

"Offside!" is my pronouncement.

"Aw, Sir, that in't fair!" he says, bitterly disappointed.

"Sorry, old mate, but you were standing nearly on the goal line."

I feel rotten because I would have been as thrilled as him if he could have scored, but the greater good must be the priority, so the goal stays disallowed. He is a resilient character though and is soon racing around after the ball again like most of the others. This is the trouble, however. At various stages of the game they are like bees round a jam jar and I have to call a halt and make them spread out to avoid trampling the ball to death.

I did say 'most' of them, because from time to time, I spot odd ones either acting about or standing nattering. At this moment, a large boy and a small one are holding a conversation like a couple of old women in a fish shop queue, oblivious to the ferment around them.

"Hey – you two – Ena and Minnie – on your bikes round the sandpit."

They look up startled, look round to make sure it's not a case of mistaken identity, the set off, moaning, up the leg-shattering slope round the long jump pit at the top of the field. This is the punishment run for anyone caught not making a contribution to the game, no matter how slight. It really is a stunner, but they have to run there and back without a pause or they go again. These two make an incongruous pair as they slog up the hill, their wheezing clearly audible down on the pitch.

3:00 pm. Half-time and a change of ends with a pep-talk for Blues about battling to the death and all that. We resume but by now, even after only twenty minutes, it's like trying to run through a bowl of custard and the ball must seem to weigh half a ton to the lads. They drag their weary legs through it, the hardest kick now only moving the ball a few feet.

They are all plastered from head to foot with our own patent brand of evil-smelling mud, which makes them look like a trayful of chocolate bobbies. One figure, nevertheless, stands out amongst them like an advert for Daz. It is Arthur Kelly of the still-immaculate green shirt under the blue bib and spotless white shorts, picking his way like a stork along the dry bits at the edge of the pitch. He is a useful player so it's hard to understand his lack of involvement.

"Oi – Arthur Kelly!" I shout to him. "What are you doing out there – looking for your handbag?"

"Me mam sez I amp't ter get mucky," he replies sullenly.

"Your mam says WHAT!" I gasp in disbelief.

"I AMP'T TER GET MUCKY," he shouts back, under the impression that hardness of hearing rather than comprehension is my problem.

"Listen mate," I go on menacingly. "If you aren't the same colour as everybody else in five minutes, I'll use you for rolling the pitch."

He regards me rebelliously for a few seconds then, seeing that I mean it, reluctantly enters the fray. He is promptly supplied with the ball and equally swiftly squashed like a fly by a crushing tackle from the big, powerful lad, Raymond Jankowicz. As Arthur is picking himself up, dazed, drenched and horrified at the thought of what his mam will say when he gets home, Raymond is hurtling after the escaping ball. He reaches it before it goes out of play, but regrettably the question of being able to stop oneself in these conditions has not entered Raymond's head.

His feet shoot from under him as they contact the ball, and both go crashing into the bushes which fringe the pitch. His momentum carries him right through the shrubbery and down the almost sheer banking beyond. His progress is marked by a serious of minor explosions and yells, which echo in the shocked silence on the pitch until they die out altogether in a fearful hush.

We all hurry to the brink and peer over apprehensively. There is no sign of Raymond in the gloom, only the trail of destruction marked by splintered and flattened plants.

Nothing happens for what seems an age, then a set of gleaming teeth and the whites of a pair of eyes chase away the shadows as Raymond jauntily hauls himself out of the middle of a holly bush, which must have interrupted his descent.

"Thank God for that!" I murmur to myself, then call out to Raymond, "You OK?"

"Yessir – it were *real* that!" I just blink in amazement – it takes all sorts I suppose.

"Have you got the ball?" I call again as though through a loudhailer.

"No, Sir. I never seed where it went."

"Well look for it you clown – we can't play without it can we?"

"No, Sir. Sorry, Sir."

"I should think so – well don't stand there apologising, look for it and be quick about it."

Luckily, the ball, not being as heavy as Raymond, has not travelled as far and is located under a branch near the top of the bank so we are soon back in business as Raymond, quite intact, camouflaged by leaves and twigs on top of the cloying mud, drags himself back onto the field. At this precise moment, Arthur Kelly, resigned by now to the fact that he will return home in a used condition, finds himself with the ball at his feet. Fearing another attack by Raymond, he races with it as far from the aggressor as he is able. His fresh pair of legs carry him past several weary challenges and he thankfully thumps the ball past the Reds' goalkeeper, at the same time darting a terrified look over his shoulder. He need not worry – Raymond is too busy recovering his breath at the far end of the field to bother about doing anyone a mischief for the time being.

What thrills! Five minutes to go now and only a goal in it. I am as caught up in the electrifying atmosphere as anybody as the game swings, or rather lurches, from end to end.

Suddenly a new noise emerges amid the general clamour. It sounds like someone sliding on a polished floor with rubber-soled shoes.

"Phrmph—" I look round in wonderment.

"Phrmph—" it goes again.

"What on earth is it?" I say out loud – completely baffled.

"It's Martin fartin'," explains Old McDougall very matter-of-factly.

"Do you write much poetry?" I ask him innocently.

"Yer what?" he asks, scrutinizing me, obviously suspecting the taking of the mick.

"Never mind – but you're kidding me surely?"

"No, Sir," Martin Westwick enters the discussion. He is the larger of the two who recently had to go round the sandpit. He is a big, gawky, uncoordinated lad who talks, as he moves, in a strange jerky manner.

"It – 'appens – every – time – I – get – excited – and – start – running – about."

"Then I wish you would try and keep it under control," I warn him, sternly. "It isn't very polite you know."

"I – can't – 'elp – it – Sir – it – just – 'appens."

"Well I would advise you not to get excited and start running about when there's a gale blowing – otherwise you're likely to finish up in Beirut!"

"Who's – that – Sir?"

"Who's who?"

"Him – what – you – just – said."

"Him what I—Oh—Beirut! It's a where not a who, but it was only a little joke so let's get on with the game now, eh?"

"Is – it – a – place – then?"

"Yes it's a place. *Please* let's finish the game."

"Is – it – near – America? You've – been – to – America – 'aven't – you – Sir? I've – been – to – China – well – Japan – axshully – with – me – mam – and – dad – when – they – went – on – their – 'oneymoon."

"Martin—"

"We – went – on – a – boat – well – a – big – ship – really. We – went – through – Switzerland—"

"WILL YOU SHUT UP AND GET ON WITH THE GAME!"

Alarmed, he phrmphs off inarticulately away from my mounting wrath, looking for his first kick of the game.

3:15 pm. I decide that I had better blow the final whistle, which brings ragged cheers from the winners. If they don't hurry up and get showered and changed they will be late for the buses, an experience we can all do without.

It's hard to hurry though after a session in such conditions and I suddenly feel drained, so much so that little Ian Noakes shames me by shuffling and tugging his tiny form level with me. It must have been torture for his twisted little limbs in all that glue, but he grins up at me full of the joys – "That were *great*, Sir!"

"Hello, wee man," I greet him. "Enjoy that did you?"

"It were *real*, Sir! Who won?"

I have a quick look at his bib, the blue barely visible beneath its coating of dirt. What the hell though! Never mind the ball – get on with the game!

"I've got bad news for you, my son." He looks questioningly at me. "You didn't make it. Better luck next time."

"Oh well, it were good though," and his grin returns. "Race you back to the changing room, Sir."

"Hell!" I exclaim involuntarily as I realise that I am lagging behind the rest. If I don't get up front before we reach the changing rooms, there will be a few who will wander in without removing their muddy boots and that can only mean trouble from a certain source. I tell them every time, but if my concentration lapses for a moment, it's all forgotten. Sure enough, in spite of a spring that would have done credit to Sebastian Coe, I am too late. The door is open and a trail of mud across the gym floor tells its own tale. It's a stupid place to have a changing room anyway – at the far end of a gym. Still, knowing that doesn't improve matters any.

I storm across after them – "How many times do you need telling to leave your muddy footwear OUTSIDE the door before you come in?" I rave at them. "Now GET back out and leave them the other side of that door – and CARRY them," I rage as one or two start to retrace their steps, their mud-caked boots still on their feet. "It's all right for you," I continue, still nearing the sound barrier, "but it's not you that Little Al—I mean Mr Light gets on to – it's me!"

They tiptoe, abashed, outside and dump their boots but their socks are so wet that they leave a new trail on the way back as well as treading in the mud that is already there.

3:30 pm. After much argument over who has and who has not to have a shower, athlete's foot, allergy to water, incipient pneumonia etc, all having been advanced as arguments against, everyone is ready to march up to the buses. I have also had a rebuke from little Noakesy that I cheated in the race back to the changing-room because I didn't wait for him to say 'go'.

This shower business is a problem. It appals me that so many of them would be quite content to pull their ordinary clothes over all the grime which covers them from head to foot. I am adamant that all except those with a genuine excuse must have a shower. Otherwise, there would be complaints from the more fastidious homes, whereas those whose families barely notice their existence, would probably arrive at school the following day still in the same condition!

One good thing about Tuesday afternoon is that Bob Robins sees to the buses by himself. This gives me the chance to get washed and changed at leisure – a rare luxury. On this occasion, though, I had forgotten the unfinished business over the alleged shooting incident, of which I am reminded by the sight of four defiant figures standing just inside the main doors. This, of course, means that a leisurely toilet is out of the question. If I don't hurry, they will be up and away on the pretext that they thought I had forgotten them.

I don't like them standing by the main door all the same, as they can too easily blend with the crowds of other people all making their way to their transport. "I thought I told you lot to wait outside Mr Coburn's office, not littering the main entrance," I snap at them. Reluctantly, without a word, they slouch past me and up the stairs to where Clive is no doubt waiting for them.

"I'll be back in five minutes," I call after them. "That's five minutes overtime for a start. The rest is up to you."

When I get back, Clive is already there, having a few words of his own with them. We send them inside his office whilst we work out a plan of campaign. We agree, initially, to work on them all together in the hope that we can reach an early settlement. Failing that, it will be one at a time.

"Let's see where we've got to so far," I begin. "A boy has been seriously injured by a shot fired from a gun by one of you. That much you've admitted already."

"We 'ampt said nowt about no gun," interrupts Delroy belligerently.

"Yes you have," I continue as smoothly as I can, as his tone tempts providence. "*You* mentioned the gun, I didn't."

"Who does the gun belong to?" asks Clive, hoping to catch them off-guard before they have warmed up.

"There in't no gun," avers Warren with his practised air of finality.

"When are we goin' to go 'ome?" asks Charles, changing the subject.

"As I said – just as soon as you stop playing silly b's and start giving us some straight answers."

"I'm in no hurry," Clive agrees. "I was thinking of staying a couple of hours to get up to date with my office work anyway."

"A couple of HOURS!" Charles exclaims in horror. "'Ow are we gunner gerrome then?"

"No problem," says Clive sweetly, "Mr Bailey and myself will see to that, providing of course it isn't too late. I have to pick my wife up at six. I don't know about Mr Bailey."

"I mustn't be much after that because I have to go out early tonight," I add my piece to help turn the screw a bit.

"I'm not staying here that long," Delroy snarls, curling his lip and glaring sidelong as he does in his recalcitrant moods.

"You don't have any choice friend unless you intend kicking the door down and I wouldn't advise that," I warn him in a similar tone to his own. There are glares all round until finally their eyes lower and remain fixed on the floor except for an occasional stealthy glance at one another and the quivering of a smile round the mouth.

“You don’t seem to have much to say, Mr Flynn,” observes Clive, breaking the silence.

“No, Sir,” is the predictable response.

“I think he needs a new needle – this one seems to be stuck,” I remark caustically, an observation that brings stifled sniggers from the group.

4:00 pm. “Look, this is getting us nowhere fast,” Clive bursts out suddenly, throwing the pencil which he has been tapping, down on the desk in vexation and striding to the door. “The only thing we can do now is have you in one at a time, ask you the same questions and see if your stories all tally. Of course it’s going to waste more time but you all seem to have plenty of that. We’ll start with you, Warren, seeing as our information is that the gun belongs to you. The rest of you wait outside.”

He opens the door, the threesome files out into the corridor and they arrange themselves on and around the window sill. No sooner has the door closed behind them that there comes a knock on it. I snatch it open irritably, thinking that it’s one of the suspects. Instead, standing there is Lesley McLoughlin, one of the staff. She takes a step back in mock alarm at the abrupt opening of the door and the sight of my irate countenance on the other side.

“Sorry to interrupt – I didn’t realise you were busy,” she says apologetically, “but you’re wanted on the phone.”

“OK – I can manage till you get back,” says Clive in reply to my questioning look.

It turns out to be Mrs Wolveridge whose son left school last year. She wants to know what happened to the coffee table, the newspaper rack, the spatula and the standard lamp, which Steven made in woodwork before he left. How the hell do I know! I don’t take them for woodwork. Bob Robins is the fellow to ask. I explain this to her with a great show of patience but she rabbits on and on about something and nothing for ages. She is one of these women who can’t tell you what they had for supper until they have been right through the day from the time they got up.

4:15 pm. Eventually I manage to escape from her but only after saying “Well, I really must be—” at least half a dozen times. I race along the corridor and am about to dash up the stairs to Clive's office when a thought crosses my mind and I screech to a halt. As I recall it, I never asked Lesley who it was on the phone, so none of the three waiting outside the office would know. Good old Mrs Wolveridge! It's a large slice of bluff, but well worth a try.

I slowly mount the stairs with what I hope looks like a smug grin on my face. The same three are still perched on the window sill so Clive must be giving Warren quite a grilling.

"Well, well, well!" I begin, rubbing my hands together and chuckling knowingly. "If you'd told us this in the first place we could have saved all this time."

"Told you what?" growls Charles suspiciously.

"That phone call I just had was from a parent asking if we knew about the boy who was shot at lunch-time by a gun belonging to that Warren Dransfield. Apparently Warren was bragging about it this afternoon to one of your mates and he went home and told his parents – so now we know."

There is a stunned silence followed by mutterings then a crescendo of fury directed at the temporarily absent Warren.

"'Im an' 'is big gob!"

"We all said we'd say nowt to *nobody*!"

"Ah'm not tekkin' it all for 'im!"

I tell them to wait a few seconds whilst I check that Mr Coburn has finished with Warren. Of course it gives them a chance to ferment a bit more wrath and affords me the opportunity to mutter the facts into Clive's ear without Warren hearing anything.

He catches on quickly, grinning delightedly, and turns to Warren.

"Right set of mates you've got haven't you? Mr Bailey tells me that when he came upstairs just now they told him all about it – say it's your gun, you shot it, and they don't see why they should get done for something that's not their fault."

"Oh yeah!?" says Warren, a cynical smile round his mouth. "Pull the other – it's got bells on!"

It is a tense moment as I open the door and stand aside. We need not have worried. The three from outside don't let us down. They come charging in like bulls into the ring.

"You WANKER!" screams Charles at the astonished Warren. "Couldn't keep it shut could yer?"

"Ah'm gunner kill you," hisses Delroy, beside himself with rage. "You wait till we're goin' 'ome, that's all."

Luckily for us, the power of the attack combined with its unexpectedness, destroy Warren's composure instantly. There is no time for him to think about what was actually said – just the need to defend himself from the new enemy – his erstwhile friends. It's better than the pictures. Clive and I simply lean back and let it all unravel as Warren hits back at his accusers.

"Ah'm not gerrin' all t' blame," he defends himself hotly. "You shunt 'ave said nowt."

"WE shunt 'ave said nowt?" echoes Charles. "It were you who were shootin' yer gob off to—to—" he breaks off as he can't remember who it was that Warren was supposed to have split to. In turn, Warren hesitates, uncertain now of who indeed said what in the first place. There is a sudden pause as the first seeds of self-doubt begin to germinate.

Clive takes advantage of this lull in the hostilities to press home the points. "Look, we all know enough now to stop the fooling. Where is the gun now?" Nobody speaks. "OK. Who does it belong to?"

"Warren," say three voices in unison. The subject of their condemnation remains silent, restricting himself to a venomous glare in their direction.

Clive persists. "Where is the gun now?" Warren hesitates – "Go and get it," he is told in a tone that brooks no argument.

With a deep sigh he goes out of the room. We wait in silence apart from Delroy, who mutters in an almost hypnotic tone – "Ah'm gunner kick 'im in."

"Look – leave it out now will you," I feel the time has come to put matters straight. "We've kidded you. That phone call was from a friend of mine. It had nothing to do with what has happened here. We played you all off against each other because we knew you were lying. We cheated you if you like – but all's fair when you're up against people who are lying and cheating themselves."

Meanwhile, Warren has returned in time to hear the last bit and they all look at each other in dismay as their suspicions are confirmed. He lays the weapon – a powerful .22 calibre air-pistol – on the desk, and I shudder at the thought of what might have happened had the shot not been fired from such a distance.

Clive picks up the gun and tells Warren, "I'll keep this until the end of term, then you can collect it."

"You're not keepin' me gun," says Warren, his truculence returning. "Me dad bought me it."

"Does your dad know you brought it to school?" I ask him.

"No."

"Have you a licence for it?"

"No."

"You realise that you maliciously wounded a person with it which makes it, strictly speaking, a police affair."

A clamour of voices rises, from which we gather that the gun went off accidentally as they were struggling over it in an argument over whose turn it was to have a shot. The fact that it hit Young McDougall was pure mischance, or so we are led to believe. It sounds a bit thin, but we decide that the lesson seems to have been learned, so we agree to give them the benefit of the doubt on this score.

4:35 pm. I look at my watch and decide that I have had enough. "Look here, Warren – it's after half-past four. Your choices are these. Either we keep it till the end of term, *or* your father comes to school and collects it, *or* it goes to the police. Make up your mind NOW!"

"I'll ask me dad tonight" he retorts sullenly holding his hand out for the pistol.

"Oh no you don't!" I tell him. "You don't listen. It stays here with us until you come up with a satisfactory answer."

4:45 pm. At last we are ready for off. Clive and I have worked out, from studying the map, where they each live, and from that, our complement of passengers. I am fortunate to finish up with Charles and Patrick, both of whom live directly on my route home. I wouldn't care to have the other two with the atmosphere between them as it is.

After dropping each at his doorstep, I drive home with an unusual feeling of elation, much as the police chief who destroyed the Kray brothers' empire must have felt. I bet his wife never played hell with him because his tea was ruined though – ah well! All in a day's work for a crimebuster I suppose.

WEDNESDAY

13th November

9:30 am. "Sir – there's a pig in t'yard." Peter Howard's cocky grin as he looks out of the window ought to be a clue that it is not as simple as all that, but I don't catch on.

My immediate reaction is "Oh no!" At various times we have had self-styled Hell's Angels churning up the drive on stolen motorbikes, regular visits from the green-keeper of the neighbouring golf club with complaints about kids trespassing on the course, pinching balls which were actually in play and building sand castles in the bunkers. We have irate parents, we have a continual stream of stray dogs of varying degrees of hostility, but never before have we had a pig!

Already this morning I have had the shock of Andrew Miller appearing for the second day running – and after yesterday's traumas too. Then I was lucky enough to be on hand to nip in the bud what could have become a vicious clash between Stuart Parsons and Delroy de Lancey over a bicycle by the main door under my office.

Now, I swivel my chair round and propel myself out of it to the window overlooking the yard. Instead of the expected chaos, I find the place deserted. "OK – what's it supposed to be – April Fool's Day a few months early?" I say to him over my shoulder. "There's nothing there."

He slides out of his seat, still grinning irritatingly, and joins me. "Look there," he says jabbing his finger in the general direction of the parked cars, but try as I may, I still can't see a single pig. The grin changes into his party-piece, a 'Woody Woodpecker' cackle which draws laughter from the rest of his gang and brings me to the stage where I could cheerfully drop him out of the window onto his head.

"I see – it's silly b's we're playing is it? Come on then, let's all be in on the joke," I say with exaggerated patience.

"Look!" He continues jabbing insistently. "That car."

My gaze follows the direction of his finger, along the line of parked cars until I spot a police car near the end. It dawns at last. "Is that what you mean?"

"Yeah – pigs," he replies challengingly.

"You want me to ask him over here so that you can tell him what you call them?" I ask him, taking up the challenge, but before he can counter, there is a tap on the door and Bob Robins hurries in looking more serious than normal.

He comes quickly over to my desk and starts talking softly but urgently out of the corner of his mouth – "Sorry to bother you, Ben, but the police are here," I nod and he goes on. "Apparently last night some of your lads had a look round Woollies in town and started to leave with pocketfuls of goods they hadn't paid for and got themselves nicked. It sounds as though it might be Big Arthur, Andrew Miller and Jeremy Knight for starters.

"Oh blast it!" I interrupt him furiously. "I was only telling someone yesterday how well Arthur's been doing here."

"Well, I may be wrong – it was just a whisper – let's keep our fingers crossed. Which reminds me – Miss Wood says you can come over and see the officers seeing as your lads are involved and she has senior assembly to do.

"Where's Clive?"

"He's out with some of the juniors at a model exhibition in Leeds."

"I see. Well, can you ask her to give me five minutes to sort out Mary's lads? The cops can have a cup of tea and rest their feet or something."

"Will do. Shall I take this lot down with me now?"

"You might as well. I shall probably have to come across for the villains when I find out for sure who they are."

9:45 am. Bob departs taking my boys with him. On Wednesdays they spend the whole day with him in a sort of factory workshop arrangement of his own device. My girls and Mary's girls spend the morning cooking with Viv Jacques, the domestic science teacher. I have Mary's boys in the morning and all the girls in the afternoon.

I send the girls off to Viv at the same time, but before I have a chance to catch my whirling thoughts, a head pops round the door and Ian Welsh enquires, "Can we come in, Sir?"

"Yes, come in and sit down." I count a dozen as they file in. "Here, Ian, give this stuff out to everybody and get someone to give you a hand." He quickly deputes Nigel Webster, his current best friend, to give him some help in handing out the rulers, papers, pencils and crayons.

Luckily I am prepared for them, which is always advisable with this lot because if they are unoccupied for even the shortest time, they are up to mischief. I use this period weekly for giving them some idea of how to deal with everyday situations or possible emergencies which most of us would take for granted. I refer to things like giving directions clearly to strangers, using private and public telephones, using telephone and street directories, even changing a light bulb. Today we are going to learn the intricacies of wiring an electric plug.

I am really pleased with the organisation for the session. There is first the 'paperwork' comprising a duplicated sheet each with a little reading then a diagram of a plug with instructions as to the colouring of the wires which they have to draw onto the plug, getting the colours in the right order. It all sounds very simple, but believe me there is a day's work here for one or two unless they are given a fair amount of help on the way. After the paperwork comes the pièce de résistance. I have managed to bring, beg or borrow a dozen plugs, lengths of three-core wire, and screwdrivers, but that will be for after break.

I leave them with instructions, threats, and a prayer whilst I go across to the Head's office to meet the law. There is a burly Sergeant who introduces himself and his companion, a weedy PC who appears to be trying to cultivate a few straggly hairs on his top lip.

"Sorry that it's trouble, Sir," he says briskly, "but it seems there's no doubt about it that some of your lads went out on a bit of a shopping spree last night—"

"Yes I know the gist of the story," I interrupt him, not rudely I hope as he's only doing his job. "Have you got the names of the people involved?"

He fishes in his pocket for his notepad and though he must know for certain, he nevertheless reads the short list like a roll-of-honour: "Andrew Miller—Jeremy Knight—and—Luke Towers."

Not Big Arthur! Thank goodness for that! It may sound insensitive, but I find I can't waste any sympathy at the thought of the first two, but I am surprised at Luke Towers' involvement.

"Would you be good enough to bring them along so that we can ask them a few questions, Sir?"

I'm beginning to like the Sergeant who reminds me of all the stout, dependable, no-nonsense officers that we have seen depicted on television drama series over the years.

I excuse myself and go across to Bob's place. I want to go myself because if I send for them there is a chance that they might not arrive.

Bob is indignant because it's going to make a balls-up of his assembly line, as he puts it, and cause him to have to reorganise his whole day. Sorry as I am, there is nothing else for it and at least he is able to share my pleasure at the knowledge that Big Arthur is not included. So, I march the suspects out of the room followed by ribald comments from the others as we go.

Like a couple who have seen it all before, Andrew and Jeremy stroll in and collapse into a pair of easy chairs. Luke, taut as a bowstring, stands white-faced, biting his lip and twisting his fingers, speechless for the first time since I have known him.

"On your feet!" I bellow at the seated pair, keen to make it understood that I'm not one of your kid-glove operators – for the benefit of the Sergeant of course. "You'll sit down when you're told," I add for good measure.

The Sergeant takes over the controls, giving them the complete story, which he had begun for me. There are no denials. He takes his time, looking up from his chair at each of them in turn, familiar with the situation of course. Slow daft-dog grin from Andrew, half-anger from Jeremy, petrified stare from Luke, in response.

"Well, Jimmy," begins the Sergeant at length surveying Jeremy. 'Jimmy', that's a new one on me, perhaps it's his professional name. "Not exactly strangers are we?" Jeremy curls his lip and looks past the Sergeant as if this is just so much kids' stuff to him.

"Now then – Andrew Miller?" The Sergeant raises his eyebrows, looks at the other two in turn, ultimately focussing with a frown on the correct party. Receiving a nod and a dopey grin in reply he goes on. "We've met before as well haven't we?"

"Yer," says Andrew grinning at the Sergeant's boots. The thought strikes me that he's just daft enough to be really enjoying something like this.

"So you must be Luke Towers?" he turns to the ashen lad who looks to be on the verge of collapse. "I don't think we know you do we?"

This gives Luke the chance to blow his fuse at last. "NO SIR. I DINT DO NOWT. I JUST WENT WI' 'EM TO LOOK ROUND T'SHOPS. I DINT KNOW THEY WERE GUNNER TEK THINGS. I DINT TEK NOWT – HONEST!" the words gush out imploringly.

"You say you went with them to look *round* the shops. Are you sure you didn't go and look *out* for them – you know – keep a lookout in case anybody saw them?" the Sergeant asks evenly, unmoved by Luke's outburst.

"NO SIR – HONEST – THEY SAID WE WERE JUST LOOKIN'. AH WUNT ER GONE IF AH'D KNOWN THEY WERE GUNNER TEK THINGS – HONEST!"

"Did either of these two *give* you anything that they took?" the Sergeant insists.

"NO SIR – HONEST!"

Honest is not a word that I would readily use in a character reference for Luke, but I know that, though often a cheat, he is usually open about it when confronted, so I am inclined to believe his pleas at the moment. I have certainly never seen him in such an emotional state before. I feel it may be time to give him a helping hand. So far as I have been like a piece of furniture in this tableau.

"You've heard what Luke just said. What have you to say about it?" I ask, addressing Jeremy and Andrew. After a while Jeremy shrugs and mutters something inaudible.

"Pardon? I didn't hear that," I say irritably.

"'E dint tek nowt. 'E 'ad nowt ter do wi' it," Andrew replies instead.

"Is that right?" I ask Jeremy.

"Yer," he agrees sullenly. "'E 'ad nowt ter do wi' tekkin things."

"Well, Mr Bailey" says the Sergeant rising to his feet. "I don't think we need take up any more of your time. I'm afraid they'll all have to come down to the station for the formalities and we'll take it from there."

"I DON'T 'AVE TER GO DO I?" howls Luke in panic. "YOU 'EARD 'EM SAY I 'AD NOWT TER DO WI' IT."

"Sorry, old lad. You were involved even if only as a witness so you will have to come along, but things don't look as bad for you."

That slight reassurance seems to calm him a little and he allows himself to be ushered out by the PC along with the other two. The Sergeant must be reading my mind as he nods at Luke's dejected figure. "He should be all right," he says, "but it won't do any harm to have the daylights scared out of him – for future reference as you might say."

I like the Sergeant even more. We shake hands and I go back to the Mansion.

10:15 am. As I enter, Ian Welsh is doing a Douglas Fairbanks Jr, on the desk above Kermit, poking him around the head with a ruler. Enraged, I grab a ruler from the nearest desk and attack him with it.

"Why do you always pick on him?" I demand, jabbing him with the point of the ruler. "If it's a sword fight you're after come on – on guard!"

I proceed to prod him vigorously as he desperately tries to cover up the unprotected bits, all the while tottering along the row of desktops until he finally runs out of ground and, clutching despairingly at the wall, crashes to the floor. On the way down he manages to drag with him the world map, complete with strings and pins, which took me an age to put up.

This of course only adds fuel to the flame and before he has chance to decide how many bones are broken, I grab him by the ear and drag him, yelping, to his desk.

“Next time I’ll do the job properly – I’ll use a real sword. Now let me see your work,” I growl menacingly.

Groaning, he tenderly feels at the various wounds he has accumulated on his flight as I glance at his diagram.

“How long did it take you to do this?” I ask gently.

“About a minute,” he brags, looking triumphantly up at me.

“You dipstick!” I rave. “That’s typical of you – rush it off as quickly as you can then pester the life out of those who are trying to get on with their work.”

“What’s up with it?” he demands, squinting at his paper in disbelief.

“I’ll tell you what’s wrong with it – you’ve only got all the wrong wires in the wrong holes – that’s what’s wrong with it,” I tell him, in spite of being shown very simply on the diagram. “Now get your nose down and do it right. I’ll be back to look at it in five minutes.”

10:35 am. Before I can get to see any more work there is a timid knock on the door and a small figure enters nervously. He tries to communicate with me in a mouse-like voice. I get down on my knees with a request for him to speak up a bit, which brings a chorus of laughs from the class.

“MRS GAMBLE SEZ ARE YER COMIN’?” he repeats deafeningly as I overbalance, involuntarily clapping a hand to my ear at the same time. This of course causes near hysteria in the audience.

“Good grief, lad! I only said speak up a bit, not burst my eardrum.” He looks so mortified that I start again more encouragingly. “Where does Mrs Gamble want to go?”

“No, Sir,” he says, striking a happy medium in volume, “she sez are you comin’ to assembly?”

Good Lord! Amid all the confusion of the morning I have forgotten that on alternate Wednesdays I take junior assembly at 10:30 am.

Again I have to leave them to it with a threat – “You all saw what happened to friend Welsh – well if anyone else is acting the goat when I get back, he won’t live to collect his old-age pension.”

10:40 am. Hot and breathless after a dash across to the hall, I find Mrs Gamble quite composed, just about to round-off the proceedings.

"Sorry I'm late – busy morning – forgot all about it."

"That's all right," she assures me serenely. "We're nearly finished anyway," and carries on with her little chat to the congregation.

Well what the hell! Why has the silly woman dragged me all the way across here just to tell me that? All this and a lot more thoughts are passing through my mind when she breaks in with a query – "Would you like to say prayers to finish assembly for us, Mr Bailey?"

She knows! She has it all worked out! She knows all about my affliction – Lord's Prayer amnesia! It all started soon after I arrived at Lees Bank – about the second assembly in fact. I discovered halfway through the Lord's Prayer that I simply could not remember the rest of the words – at least not in the right order. Luckily for me, I looked up at the right moment and found big Susan Jankowicz serenely mouthing the words with all the fervour of a hot-gospeller. She unwittingly guided me home and ever since I have – unknown to anyone else either – relied on her on every occasion.

Alas! At the junior assembly there is nobody to provide this service. I have to give the lead but once we get past 'as in heaven—' I am lost. Usually Mrs Gamble's voice can be clearly heard, but this time she is silent and we grind to a halt. Everyone looks up as if woken from a hypnotic trance and blinks in the light.

"Hah – that caught you all out didn't it?" I exclaim as convincingly as possible though a glance out of the corner of my eye confirms that maybe Mrs Gamble is not at all convinced. "I wondered if you could finish the prayer without me," I press home the point. "Does anyone know the rest?" hoping fervently that some kind soul will come to my rescue.

"Yessir – I can," pipes up Ralph Moreton from the third row. A grand little lad is young Ralph – these are the exact words that run through my mind as I beam paternally at him. Actually he is a fine lad – a real character. He has the most comical manner of speaking – all the solemnity and exaggerated grammatical correctness of an answerphone. His parents obviously pay him the compliment of speaking to him in an adult manner and he can certainly hold his own in conversation with anyone. The reason he is with us is that, sadly, at the age of nine, he can scarcely read or write a word. "Would you like me to continue or would you prefer me to recommence?" he asks, warming to the responsibility.

" I think it might be preferable if you were to recommence," I tell him. When you are talking to Ralph, you find yourself spontaneously adopting the same style. "I think it would be a good idea if Ralph says the prayer and we all join in with him don't you?" I enquire of the congregation. Much nodding of heads and murmurings of assent greet this suggestion. His reedy voice guides us unerringly through and I judge this an ideal moment to make an exit, rather like a visiting archbishop, amid waves and farewells.

10:50 am. It's a change to get a cup of tea before the urn runs dry and I take it across to my room. To my relief the room is empty and there is no more debris than that normally found after a session with Mary's lot. There is, however, the world map hanging forlornly by one corner like the saloon door after a wild-west brawl. I repair it with blu-tack as well as I can but it still doesn't look right as it now has a couple of tears in it.

11:00 am. Right on the dot they file in eager to get to grips with the practical side of things.

"Right men – gather round and I'll show you how to do the job *properly*. Remember, there is nothing more dangerous than a badly or wrongly-wired plug – it can *kill*! Are you listening, Ian Welsh?"

"Yes, Sir."

"What can it do?"

"Kill, Sir."

"Correct. Remember, it's like me – if you don't treat it properly it can be dangerous."

Impressed, they gather round. I meticulously shave the wire and go with elaborate care through each stage, relating the whole procedure to their diagrams as a back-up in case their memory fails, as it surely will in at least half the cases.

"You can work in pairs to help each other and when one has finished let me know and I'll come and have a look. One of each pair can come and collect your tackle."

They line up and receive a length of wire, plug, screwdriver, and miniature Stanley knife borrowed from the art room. Each rushes off, absolutely thrilled at the chance to do something that demands such a high level of technical skill.

While they are sorting out the gear and arguing over turns, I nip over to Ian Welsh to check on whether he has finished his diagram to my satisfaction.

"Excellent," I pronounce. "Wouldn't it make life a lot easier if you did something like this in the first place instead of acting like the village idiot most of the time?"

He just grins which doesn't really answer my question but I move off and leave him to it. There is a breathless hush in the class as ten pairs of hands unite with ten sets of brains to perform the task, which looked so simple a few minutes earlier.

"Finished, Sir!" They haven't been at it long but Ian Welsh's voice rings out confidently to break the industrious tension.

"Oh yes," I reply sceptically. "I can just imagine what it will be like done so quickly. I wish you would *take care* instead of dashing things off in such a hurry and making a pig's ear of it."

I go and examine his efforts. Perfect! No bare wires showing and when I open it up, everything is neatly tucked away and screwed up in the right spot.

"Well – I have to admit this is absolutely bang-on. Good lad."

I hold it up for public examination and everyone agrees enviously that, as a technician, Ian Welsh is tops. "Change over then and let Nigel have a go. Unscrew it all and start right from the beginning then it's all fair."

It seems to be proving a huge task for some of them even with combined brain power. The table where Akhtar Singh and partner are working is covered with a confetti-like assortment of bits of chopped wire and though there is plenty of endeavour, nobody seems to be making much headway.

"Finished, Sir!" Again it is the dynamic-duo who are first past the post. I go over and have a look – perfect again, but being suspicious by nature and a student of form, something strikes me as being not quite right.

"Have you done it this time, Nigel?" I ask pleasantly enough.

"Yes, Sir," he replies with a winning smile.

"You really have done a very good job on it," I continue admiring the end product of his dexterity. "Tell you what – most of the others are struggling a bit so I think it might be a good time for them all to gather round and watch how easy it can be when you really think about it."

The smile recedes like water going down a plughole. "I'll do it, Sir," volunteers Ian Welsh hurriedly, bringing a look of sheer gratitude from his partner.

"No thank you," I insist. "We'd much rather watch Nigel do it again just to prove that it wasn't beginner's luck."

"Ooh—I don't think I could do it with everybody watching – it makes me feel nervous."

"You'll be all right once you get started," I assure him. I rapidly dismantle it and place the parts in front of him on the table. He views them with utter dismay and screws up the corners of his mouth.

"Come on," I encourage him, handing him the screwdriver, which he views as if it were a live snake. "My word you have got a short memory. Anybody would think you'd never seen a screwdriver before."

Seconds pass and still he keeps his head down, not moving a muscle.

"Just start like you did last time," I suggest, and he looks up at me, dumbly. "You haven't a clue have you?" I ask him in as even a tone as I can manage. He shakes his head miserably as I turn to his partner. "Did you fix the plug both times?"

"Yes, Sir," he answers, delighted at last that his genius has been recognised.

"Bonehead!" I snap at him. "What use is it to him for you to do the thing twice. The idea is for you *both* to be able to handle the job. Knowing him he probably never even watched. Now seeing that *you* are so good at it will you please tell *him* how to do it so that we can all see. No – *tell* him how to do it," I break in as he picks up the tools and starts to assemble the parts for a third time.

To his credit he makes a fair job of instructing his partner. Nigel Webster's concentration span is about as long as a spent matchstick but though Ian's vocabulary is not up to a full verbal breakdown of the task, he manages by gestures and monosyllabic grunts to achieve a reasonable result. Such a feat is often proved to be beyond the capabilities of professionals in Nigel's case. There are a few stingy wires here and there but nothing that is downright dangerous.

"There – that wasn't too bad was it?" I ask the drained, sweating Nigel. His look of relief is quite comical. I turn to Ian – "You did a sound job there, mate. Play your cards right and I could get you a job on the staff." Alarmingly for him, he blushes and looks every way but straight ahead. "All right – you've seen it can be done quite easily by a complete beginner. Now time's running out so I'll give you five minutes to get your act together then I'm coming round to look at them."

11:35 am. "Righto then – ready or not I'm coming!" Actually I have given them ten minutes – ten minutes of frantic activity the like of which I have never seen from this bunch before. So, whatever the results, I can hardly fault them on effort.

I move from table to table feeling like a judge at a WI flower show. Some are passable and receive muted compliments; others have to be condemned on the grounds of safety.

Little Akhtar Singh's table is now a mass of chopped-up wire, while his plug has three skinny bare wires, each with a minute blob of coloured plastic on the end, sticking out of the hole. It has a look of rigor mortis about it. "What are you going to do with this lot?" I ask him, indicating the diced wire on the desk.

"Ve run out of vire, Sir," he explains apologetically whilst his partner, the enormous David Goodyear looks down reproachfully on him implying that it really had nothing to do with *him*.

"You can say that again," I agree. "Still you should be able to get a job in an Indian take-away if you can chop vegetables as well as that – so long as you don't offer to do any electrical work for them." He grins sheepishly as David shakes his head at him, the unspoken message clear – "Another fine mess you've gotten me into, Stanley!"

Roy Slade and Peter Darnley are a bright pair! Peter is a fine games player but his academic achievements could be recorded on the back of a postage stamp. Much the same can be said of Roy except that he can't play games even. Still, their plug looks impressive – just a bit of separation showing as the wires enter the plug but nothing bare. However, when I open it up, all three wires are fixed in the wrong holes!

"The diagram shows you the colour of the wires and the initials of the holes they are supposed to go in," I explain wearily, pointing from diagram to plug. They look from one to the other, expressionless.

"Has your mum got two hands?" I ask Roy. He nods, mystified. "And one head?" Again he nods. "Well she'd be lucky if she had any of them left if she plugged this into a socket. They'd probably get blown off!" They both wriggle uncomfortably at the thought as the rest of the group hoots with unsympathetic laughter.

And so to Kermit! Kermit is the brains of the partnership between himself and Albert Barker – need I say more! Albert says very little and what he does say doesn't make much sense. If you happen to overlook him, not a difficult thing to do at busy times, he will sit for hours content to do absolutely nothing. I was a bit careless allowing him and Kermit to team up but nothing ventured, nothing gained.

Their plug rattles like a Salvation Army money-box as I pick it up and turn it over to take it apart, the top falls off and clatters across the floor followed by the screw – so far so good! This reveals all the wires in one lump. Whoever it was (perm any one—) has attempted to stuff all three wires into the same hole. The result has been a failure but all three bare wires are nevertheless intertwined.

I look in horror at the abortion. Even the rest of the gang can see that it's a real classic and snigger meanly, unwilling to laugh out loud though in case they are called on to repair it.

"Kermit," I say with my usual air of long-suffering when faced with one of his masterpieces. "Do you know what would happen if you plugged this in?"

"No, Sir," he beams in anticipation though.

"It would probably blow your house into the middle of the next street!"

This provokes an orgy of derision. They all roll about with tears in their eyes. Kermit himself laughs so much that he falls backwards off his chair, kicking the table and all its contents over.

12:00 noon. I usually set Mary's lads on clearing away early because it normally takes at least a quarter of an hour to recover all the apparatus we started off with. Today is not too bad though, except that we have to abandon the search for some of the vital bits from Kermit's plug but that is nothing fresh.

Lunch is a bit of a dull affair today as the seven dwarfs are on a trip (the one-day variety). Their empty table looks so forlorn it gives me quite a pang. Added to that, a morning with Mary's boys and the prospect of an afternoon with her girls has a rather numbing effect on the spirits.

12:30 pm. I wander over into the yard where all seems quiet. It's remarkable how the weather is reflected in the moods of our children. When it's windy they go wild, when it's rainy they are at their most troublesome because they are kept indoors. In the snow and ice it's all hell let loose. Hot sunny weather produces an abnormal number of hot tempers, heated arguments and bitter fights.

Today has become dull and cool and everyone is slouching morosely around. There isn't even an organised game of football, just a desultory kick-around in a corner.

Indoors, the same applies. The inertia is uncanny. However, taking advantage of it I retire to my office, switch on the radio and settle down to a cup of coffee and the newspaper. It shouldn't be long before the complaints start rolling in—

1:30 pm. A clatter of female voices jars me into consciousness. I can never remember falling asleep in this way before and a glance at my watch tells me that I have been 'out' for half an hour.

I feel cheated in a way because it doesn't seem as if I have been able to take full advantage of the respite. Still, I must have needed it.

The noise is coming from Mary's girls who are milling around outside. I let them into the classroom and they quickly occupy their usual places.

They are a weird bunch who spend most of their time snapping and snarling at each other like a pack of vixens. Yet there is a sort of symbiotic relationship between pairs of them, a bit like Pixie and Dixie except that theirs appear to be based more on mutual loathing than admiration.

I use this afternoon for individual work with my girls, whom I see very little during the week. They are each allowed to work on a project of their own choice whilst I go around interrupting them periodically to put in a little extra time on chronic weaknesses in their work.

The term 'project' can be used to cover a multitude of sins but I make sure that it is something purposeful rather than merely cutting pictures of pop stars out of trashy magazines.

Mary's girls come with their own set work, so as far as I am concerned all I do is correct it, give them a helping hand when needed, but – most important of all – keep them from tearing lumps off each other.

I settle for five minutes behind my own desk to recover my wits which are still swimming around in my head after the unaccustomed nap, and to let them settle into a rhythm of work or otherwise.

It doesn't take long. "Gerrup there you silly bag!" Carla Spavin starts pushing Ann Sissons's belongings into a space further along the table. "I can't do my writing with you right up here." She has a point as she is in an 'acceptable' place along the side of a table whilst Ann, for some reason, is sprawled across the corner of the table with herself and her belongings tangled up with Carla.

"There in't any more room," she mewls plaintively. Her voice is slightly slurred and quavery, partly the result of regular drug-dosage, partly, I feel a family trait. Her cousin Martin in my class, is a bit dozy as well. Be that as it may, however, she once did have a fit of some kind in infancy and ever since has been on drugs to prevent a recurrence. Most of us feel that she might benefit from some gradual withdrawal for a period to see what happens, but we are not the experts. As it is, it seems a pity that a good-looking, smart girl has to go through life in this doped condition.

"Course there is you daft cow – sit this side," snaps Carla, waving an arm to indicate the wide-open spaces to her right. In contrast to Ann, Carla has a voice that could peel potatoes.

"The sun gets in my eyes there," claims Ann.

"There isn't any sun today you fool," Carla retorts scathingly and starts to pick up Ann's things. Ann grabs at them and a tug-of-war of such ferocity ensues that the papers are bound to be torn unless something is done quickly.

"STOP IT AT ONCE!" I bawl at them, so loud that I even make myself jump. The effect on them is stunning. They both turn towards me, open-mouthed and quietly lower the objects of their struggle onto the table, and continue to stare at me. I think they must have given me up for dead before that. I am just beginning to congratulate myself on quelling the potential riot so effectively when the rest of the pack weigh in.

"She's thick 'er," declares Teresa Ryan with great authority, but before she can develop the thesis, Ruth Tinker's waspish voice cuts in.

"She's always causing 'er bother 'er."

"Who is?" enquires Carla glaring dangerously at each of them. These three would be naturals for any production of *Macbeth* if they could only read the script.

"She is," they chorus, nodding vehemently in Ann's direction, "that Sissons – she never minds 'er own business," adds Ruth to clarify the situation.

"I wondered how long it would be before the neighbours started peeping round the curtains," I join in scornfully. "You two could start a riot in an empty house! Now get on with your work and that means all of you."

They bend to their various tasks, glancing up slyly from time to time to dart malicious grins at one another. Mary has this all day except on the few occasions when someone else takes over to give her a breather. Thank goodness mine aren't like that very often!

"What you going to do about 'er?" asks Shirley Baker pointing at Carol Crawford. What was it I was just saying about my lot?

"Oh for goodness sake! Don't get like the other group. I thought *you* had a bit more about you than that." I know that she is referring to Carol's late arrival yesterday, which I have conveniently forgotten in the hope that it might go away.

The appeal is ignored. Normally any unfavourable comparison with the lower forms of life to be found on the other side of the landing has the desired effect, but not this time – apparently the matter is considered to be of too great a principle to be sidetracked. "You said you were goin' to do summat about 'er," she persists.

"Well I haven't seen her since it happened," I protest.

"You saw 'er this morning when you did the register."

"Yes but I can't remember everything. Look at what happened this morning – would you have remembered?" I am sure I've scored a point here, but it is returned like an overhead smash.

"Course I would! Anyway she's here now so you can tell 'er."

There is a murmur of agreement from the rest of my girls – the ones who are interested that is – and a clatter of pencils, needles and other objects as Mary's crew come to attention, sadistically anticipating a good old row.

The thought often strikes me that politicians could learn a great deal from our pupils in spite of all their shortcomings (the shortcomings of our pupils that is). Our kids have a stunning sense of immediacy, which our rulers could profitably emulate. As it is, I am struggling at the moment and there is no way off this particular hook.

Carol, thankfully, sets the ball rolling for me. "I couldn't help it could I?" which is actually no help at all but it does at least give me something to start talking about.

"Why couldn't you help it?" I ask. I am always in difficulties with this one. She has a very unstable and sometimes violent home life, if we are to believe all we hear. I don't want to make things any harder for her, but if a firm line is not adopted she tends to take advantage.

"Me mam din't wek me up when she went to work did she? So I slept in."

"You should go to bed earlier," I suggest, thinking that it might be a basis for agreement, but this is promptly shot to pieces.

"I went to bed at nine o'clock din't I?"

"Then there's no good reason why you can't wake up in good time. Have you got an alarm-clock?"

"I never 'ear it do I?"

"Well your mum's just going to have to make sure that you are up and ready every time she leaves for work."

"She always forgets dun't she?"

"I wish you would stop asking me a question at the end of everything you say – it's most irritating."

"It's way I talk in't it?"

"I wish you'd get out of the habit then and do yourself a favour – anyway this is getting us nowhere fast. Look – let me put it this way – you and your mum are going to have to work something out between you because if it happens again I shall take your bus pass from you and you will have to come on the school bus."

"I'm not comin' wi' t'littluns," she fumes. "I shan't come at all so—"

Whatever she is going to finish with never gets out so I have to resume the battle. "You know what it means if you start that again." There were threats a few months ago when she was persistently absent that a care order might be made. She knows what I mean and looks down, her eyes beginning to redden. This is not what I want so I try to compromise. "Look – all you have to do is show me that you are grown-up enough to take the responsibility for getting here on time. Nine-thirty, NINE-THIRTY! Some people have to be at work at half-past six and you can't even manage it three hours later. Good grief! Surely it's not asking too much. Now – what about it – are you going to make the effort or not?"

"I suppose so."

"And you accept the alternative?"

"Eh?"

"I mean – you understand that if you keep on coming late and deliberately missing out on things you don't like or want to do, then you will lose you bus pass?"

"Suppose so."

I am glad to leave it there because it's obvious we are getting near the red line. There – I can proudly say that I have exercised a bit of democracy, which I claim, not always with justification I must admit, that we practise in our class. I turn to Shirley for her endorsement of my masterful handling of the situation, and blow me if she and Christina aren't leaning over her, murmuring comfortingly in her ear, and shooting me looks which could kill at fifty paces! Marvellous isn't it. They start it all off, then they become the angels of mercy and as usual I am the wicked uncle.

I get up and go on a tour of inspection leaving them to their mutual consolation. It never fails to amaze and amuse me how quickly they fall in and out of harmony with one another. One minute they can be screaming abuse and fighting, the next they have their heads together drooling over a picture in a magazine.

I have a good look at Louise's work. She is busy writing a story for entry in a competition. Apart from correcting one or two spelling mistakes there is absolutely nothing to criticise. I feel helpless where Louise is concerned. Work of this standard should have a better setting but there is no outlet for it apart from personal satisfaction. Still, she might win the competition. I must make sure that I do my best to persuade her parents to allow her to go on the one-year course run by the polytechnic for our type of pupil. Hopefully her ability will be noticed and she may be allowed extended facilities for her abilities to flourish in the more cloistered atmosphere of further education.

Paradoxically, at the other side of the table, Carla, whose nature is the exact reverse of Louise's, is also doing work of a high quality. She is doing an exercise from an English textbook used as preparation for O-levels. How on earth she has managed to reach this point in the frenetic atmosphere of Mary's class, taking into account also her own volatile nature, is a miracle. The difference between her and Louise however is that Louise can initiate her own tasks and carry them out with minimal supervision and prompting. Carla on the other hand lacks this ability to work on her own initiative and is easily distracted. Nevertheless, whilst she will never be an academic, the ability to do work of this standard is surely an indication that there is a future for her, if only we could make her socially more acceptable at the same time.

At the side of her, Ann is gazing vacantly across the room. In contrast to Carla, her academic expectations are virtually nil. She is at present attempting some sort of collage with an assortment of fibres, milk-bottle tops, paint, glue, all waiting on the table for her daydream to end. She doesn't even notice as I stand beside her and lean across for a closer inspection of what she has started to do.

"WHAT YOU GAWPIN' AT LASS!" Ruth Tinker's gale-force yell makes everyone jump as it shatters the unaccustomed peace. It is directed at Ann, whose glazed eyes eventually focus in bewilderment on her accuser but she says nothing.

"What on earth is wrong with you?" I ask irritably. "Everybody's working away quietly then you go off like an air-raid siren.

"She's not workin', she's starin' at me – stupid bitch!" Ruth insists angrily.

"You know what happens to people who think everyone is staring at them don't you?" I ask her.

"Yer what?" she says suspiciously.

"I said you know what they do with people who imagine that other people are staring at them."

"What?"

"They take them away."

Shrieks and cackles greet this observation whilst Ruth, enraged, half-turns away from me muttering viciously to herself.

"You – stupid bitch." Ann, back in the land of the living again, throws this one in with a delighted grin. She is not sharp enough to think up her own barbed comments or rude names, nor even to remember ones from previous occasions. What she does instead is to field the abuse directed at her by others and throw it back. Not very original but it pleases her.

Unfortunately her timing is not always perfect and on this occasion it only adds fuel to the flames. Ruth, humiliated by being laughed at by her cronies for what I said to her, is unable to cope with Ann's follow-up. She jumps up and throws her needlework to the floor then stamps out of the room. It seems for a moment as if she is going to attack Ann, but instead she just storms straight past her.

I don't bother to go after her. When she has got used to the idea that nobody is particularly interested in her tantrums, she will be back.

After this minor flurry everyone promptly resumes and I have to smile to myself. In a more sensitive and sophisticated environment, such an occurrence would be an outrage, shocking and horrifying people and often leaving a psychological mark for some time, but here we just accept it and carry on. I think if more were made of these frequent incidents, pupils would come to realise what a powerful weapon they had and progress, even as we know it would come to a standstill. Far better I think to minimise them, then they usually have no more effect than April showers.

2:30 pm. Break – and although I have just made the point that these are no more than minor happenings, they still have a cumulative effect and the mid-afternoon break appears like half-time in a tempestuous football match.

2:45 pm. Back they all come including, of course, Ruth, full of beans as if nothing had happened. There are just one or two more people to visit on my first round and I am about to make a beeline for Maria Peters when a familiar voice arrests me.

"*You've* made Carol cry." With a sinking feeling I turn to face the Les Dawson reception committee in customary pose – arms folded, heads at various angles. Shirley and Christina are standing like sentries at each side of Carol's chair. She is still red-eyed, but from the look of her, it must be some time since she shed a tear and then, probably only at the insistence of the other two.

"*I've* made her cry – I like that!" I retort a little petulantly. "If I remember it correctly, it was *you* two who forced the issue. I might have handled it quietly between the two of us some time but no – *you* had to *see* that it was done so don't heap all the blame on me."

"You wouldn't have done anyway."

"You can't have it both ways. I did it your way because you insisted and I like to think I try to do the right thing – well, whenever I can."

"You didn't have to make her *cry*."

"I can't help it if she cries easily."

"I DO NOT!" shouts Carol, springing to a life of her own at last, little sign in her voice of the tragedy that she is supposed to be undergoing.

"Anyway I've heard quite enough about it. I've said what's to be done and you know that when I say something I mean it. So, now we let the matter drop OK?" I tell them all with what I hope is an air of finality.

"You said I'm just like your daughter," says Carol coming down an octave and apparently shooting off obliquely.

I can just about see the relevance however – I once told Carol that she reminded me very much of my own daughter – same age, same temperament, same cunning. That was why – I told her at the time – I was up to all her tricks and kept a firm grip as well as it was possible to do. "That's right, still the same," I assure her.

"I like your wife – she's lovely," Carol resumes very matter-of-factly."

I don't know where all this is leading us but it's in a much more amiable vein so I decide to go along with it for a while. "Why thank you," I reply graciously.

"Yeah, she's not like you – you're a right misery. We can't do owt wi' you."

"Thank you again. If you mean you can't do just as you like without any control then I completely agree with you."

"Well—yer not *too* bad I s'pose," she says, screwing up her eyes as if to pierce the armour-plated exterior more easily.

"Oh please – *please*, no compliments. I don't think I could cope with it." It is beginning to dawn on me during this cosy chat that Carol, Shirley and Christina are all sitting back comfortably, at peace with the world now, doing absolutely sweet nothing! Carol and Shirley are supposed to be catching up on the news week, which they missed on Monday through being at the playgroup and Christina is making up an illustrated menu for Mrs Jacques. "It has just struck me that whilst we are having this fascinating discussion about my family, you three are having a really soft time. Remind me some time to tell you about my Aunt Nellie's bad back and Auntie Clarice's feet, but for now can we get down to some work – PLEASE. If you haven't finished when it's time to go home, it will be time for the *others* to go home if you follow me."

They all apply themselves abruptly to the task with exaggerated earnestness and I go off to complete the circuit.

As I approach Maria, her eyes begin to slide guiltily from side to side and she starts to guide something furtively under the table. Guilty is the word – I can smell it a mile away. I should have been aware that if Maria had been her normal self, she would have been into the pre-break fracas with all guns blazing. It can't have been work that prevented it that's for sure, and now that she has surreptitiously removed whatever was in front of her, the desk-top is bare – need I say more?

"Working hard are we?" She bites her lip and averts her eyes. "Come on then – let's see it," I request, hand outstretched.

"See what?" is the inevitable reply.

"Whatever you have just pushed under the table. If you had desks with lids you might possibly have been able to slip it in there and I couldn't have proved a thing, but as it is, you can't hide things under a flat table can you? So it must be in your hand. May I have it please?"

She lifts both hands and turns them about to reveal the contrasting white palms – but nothing else naturally.

"Or on your knees of course – stand up please." She does so to the accompaniment of a clatter of something on the floor. I squat down and recover a magazine of some kind. Lifting it up to the light reveals the most ghastly horror-comic imaginable – the whole business – people with green skins, dismembered, decapitated and decomposing corpses – no wonder the live ones are green!

"Is this all you've been doing since the start of the afternoon?" I demand crossly.

"There's nowt else to do," she answers with that infuriating curl of the lip, and a flickering of the eyes sideways to see how the neighbours are reacting. It probably has a nervous origin but it still makes it difficult for me to be pleasant to her, which is probably why we never seem to have even the beginnings of an amiable relationship. The claim that she makes only makes matters worse.

"Is your diary up to date?"

"No."

"Have you finished Monday's news?"

"No."

"Have you asked for the bag of coins as I've told you to do?"

"No."

"Well then, how DARE you try to make out that you have nothing to do? There's enough with what I've just mentioned to keep *you* busy for a week at the rate *you* apply yourself."

I have been trying, with conspicuous lack of success, for a few weeks now, to get her to add up the contents of a bag of coins correctly. I have a number of these bags, all containing around, but not exactly fifty pence. One has, say, forty-six pence, another fifty-three pence. This is of course, to prevent them from guessing the amount.

I look at her diary, a small notebook they all have to keep religiously as a self-discipline exercise, just half a page for each day. I see that no entry has been made since the weekend. "All right, get this filled in for Monday and Tuesday for a start." The lip curls again and I resist the urge to throttle her.

I move on to Pixie and Dixie who are working like slaves – on a joint project of course. They are surrounded by mutilated periodicals, scissors, glue, newspaper and a stack of cut-out pictures. I am pleased to see that they are also doing some writing, presumably to explain the content of the pictures. These they are sticking onto a large piece of poster-paper and surrounding with a neatly-ruled border.

"Hey – this looks good!" I greet the conjoined heads, which give them the appearance of Siamese twins. "What exactly is it that you're doing?" I ask, trying to manoeuvre myself into a position where I can see the whole picture.

The two heads rise sufficiently for the eyes to meet mine – "Fishing," whispers Dixie demurely.

"Fishing!" I look in amazement at the evidence – not a rod in sight, not a solitary line, hook, maggot or fish. The effect of my comment on the two girls however, is galvanic. They both erupt with laughter, but downwards so that only the tops of their heads and trembling shoulders are visible.

After a short while, they compose themselves and look up again, still with the quiverings of smiles at the corners of their mouths. This time it's Pixie who explains, but still with a strength which would not disturb a cobweb – "Flashing."

"Flashing!" I again echo incredulously. Admittedly there are a few meagrely-clothed young ladies on view, but I never knew that women did it, much less that it merited close study of this kind.

This time, Pixie and Dixie almost have convulsions. Overt emotion is not their style, but here they are, gurgling and choking to such an extent that I am becoming alarmed for them. Eventually it all subsides after drawing in the rest of the sorority who shriek and cackle outrageously without really having the foggiest idea of what's going on. Just so it couldn't be said that they missed an opportunity.

"NO – FASHION!" is the ultimate joint explanation of the project. By combining their voices, the volume becomes about that of the normal conversational level of the average individual.

"Oh sorry! I could see that it's very good but I couldn't connect it with either of the things I thought you said." They look at each other with relief that it's all over and they can resume their normal untroubled existence. "You really are putting it together well," I tell them in genuine admiration. "These pictures are beautifully presented. Let me have a look at your writing."

They lean apart briefly to allow me to pick up the squares of paper. Contact is immediately renewed.

I'm afraid that it's something of a case of 'After The Lord Mayor's Show—', the writing neat but the spelling atrocious. "Tell you what," I suggest to them. "Why not do your writing in your jotters first, let me check the spellings then you can write it out on these squares of paper and it will be perfect – how about that?"

They nod their heads slowly – whether they *really* agree or not I don't know, but in any event they would be unlikely to express disagreement. I make a few alterations to the pieces of writing, which they haven't already stuck onto the master-sheet and they painstakingly but contentedly set about writing it all out again.

Some may disagree with this as a practice but I feel that it is the best way. I don't want to have people mocking their work if it goes on display and the important thing is that *they* have made the initial effort. My function is correction and help, and that is exactly what is happening here.

I move round to Maria for a progress check. When I arrive, she is simply sitting with her pen resting on the paper. Each page of the diary was ruled in half before we began to write in them, so they knew exactly how much room they were allowed for each day – no more, usually less. In Maria's case, Monday consists of two and a half lines (out of eight), Tuesday – which is less of a distant memory – merits three, and now she sits, stumped.

When we first started the diaries they were completely baffled. The waking day consists of something over twelve hours, therefore it must take well over that time to write about it – was the reasoning. So I told them that it was simply a matter of remembering one or two things that stood out in the mind as they thought back over the day, and jotting it down very briefly. Most of them now have the knack but one or two, Maria among them, just cannot grasp the concept.

I look at what she has written and can hardly make out a word it's so untidy. "Have you finished or are you having a breather?" I ask her.

"Finished." I wish I could learn her mastery of the art of the terse reply. I think that she knows more swear words than normal ones if listening to her in her unguarded moments is any guide. I once collared her in the playground after one particularly spectacular mouthful, and forbade her to talk at all if she could not do so without swearing. According to Joe Johnson, who was her class teacher at the time, she didn't speak for about three days!

"Tell me what it says will you – then we're both on the same wavelength," I say with what I hope is great tact.

She looks blankly at the scribble in front of her, makes a couple of false starts and smirks in embarrassment.

"What's this bit about Monday – what did you do on Monday?" I point haphazardly at the page.

"Went home and lit the fire—"

"Yes."

"Then I put the washing on and made the tea."

"Were you by yourself?"

"No."

"Who else was at home?"

"They was our Cissy and our Curtis and our Franny."

"Are they all at school."

"Yes."

"How old are they?"

"Our Cissy's six, our Curtis is seven an' our Franny's ten."

"How do they get home?"

"On they own."

"Doesn't anyone meet them?"

"No – me mam and dad's at work."

I turn to Tuesday. This conversation has been a good thing. I almost forgot that, from what I have heard, she is nothing but a glorified servant and baby-minder at home. No wonder she is so sour when she comes to school and someone else starts to push her around.

"Tell me about Tuesday," I go on, resting my finger on the page.

"I done the shoppin' after school. Then I gone home and lit the fire and started tea—"

"OK – I get the picture. You can leave your diary for now and we'll have a shot at counting the money." I would like to think she has done her best with the diary, but you can never be sure with Maria. She has very limited potential, but at the same time there is certainly a low level of interest.

I produce a bag of money with forty-seven pence in it and give it to her. Reluctantly she empties the coins onto the table and begins to push them around aimlessly.

"YER PIG – YER SILLY PIG – I'LL KICK YER 'EAD IN!" Once again everybody jumps ten feet at an almighty outburst from the other side of the table. Ann is standing with one hand on the back of her chair, the other clutched apprehensively to her mouth. Carla, who is responsible for the disturbance, is sitting fiercely grasping the table with both hands, her face twisted in a mixture of rage and pain.

"What the blazes is going on!" I demand.

"That silly pig 'it me with a chair – I'm gunner smash 'er face in!" Carla's explanations are usually very much to the point.

This one needs stepping on as quickly as possible as we have had enough of the violent verbals for one afternoon. "For a start – you can cut out that kind of talk and threats. Goodness knows what your mother would think if she could hear you using language like that." I turn to Ann and ask her, "Now what's all this about you hitting Carla with a chair?"

She has got over her initial alarm at the fury of Carla's reaction and now, with her usual rather dozy grin, says, "I were only getting' up an' I banged 'er leg wi' me chair. I were laughin' at Adrienne and Caroline so much I wanted to wee. I moved me chair so's I could get out to go t'lav. I didn't do it on purpose."

"Silly pig!" snorts Carla unforgivingly.

"Enough!" I snap, pointing threateningly at her. "Go on Ann – for heaven's sake go to the toilet and we can have some peace for a while."

"Din't do it on purpose." The words float back faintly as she drifts through the door.

I turn my attentions back to Maria. "How far have you got then?" She simply fixes her eyes on the pile of coins, opens her mouth, and moistens her lips with her tongue. I try to sound encouraging – "Come on, pick them up and start counting – try to remember how I showed you last time."

The coins range in value from ten pences down to half-pences. Hesitantly she picks up one of the tens. "How much is that?" I ask her.

"Ten p."

"Right – what are you going to do with it?" She puts it down and picks up another. "Look – you go right through, count them all whilst I'm watching then tell me how much there is and I won't say a word till you've finished," I tell her, fascinated by this process.

She picks up the coins in turn then returns them to the pile, alternately closing her eyes and soundlessly moving her lips. This goes on for an uncomfortable length of time until I am forced to break my pledge. "How much is there so far?"

She looks blankly at the pile again then shrugs – "Dunno."

"How do you know that you don't keep picking up the same coins?" This time she wrinkles her nose and shrugs one shoulder without replying.

"If you go on like this you'll be there forever. Look – let me show you again how to arrange it. You'd all better come round and watch this. It won't do any harm." Whilst the rest of the gang are making the most of their chance to cause as much noise and confusion as they can, dragging chairs around and barging into each other, I ask Maria, "How do you go on with your money when you go shopping so often – don't you ever get it wrong then?"

"I jus' give 'em it an' they give me change."

"But how do you know whether it's right or not?" Again a casual lift of the shoulders dismisses the problem. I suppose it must be all right or her mother would kick up a fuss – perhaps she doesn't have any more idea than Maria, which I find hard to believe. Still, if that is the case, there must be some contented shopkeepers in their area.

The stampede to surround the table eventually subsides but not without the usual jostling, elbowing and glares, which are best left to die a natural.

I spread the coins out so that they are all separate from one another and decide that it obviously makes most sense to use Maria for the demonstration. "Now Maria – what do we do first?"

A lengthy pause followed by, "Dunno," as I expected.

"Anybody?"

"Put 'em in different piles," says Shirley promptly.

"Good. Which first?"

"Tens," from Christina. As usual it's the same ones who come up with the ready answers. It would be better if it were the other end of the pack, but it is good to know that not all the seed fall on stony ground all the time.

"Now Maria – pick up all the ten pences. You know which they are don't you?"

She gives me a shrivelling look then begins awkwardly trying to lift a coin by its edge. This of course is very difficult at the best of times but when there is emotional pressure as well, the task is double hard. Matters are not helped by the derisive comments of her 'friends' either.

I sense that flash point is approaching so I intervene. As I have said, she has a volatile nature and so far this afternoon she has been remarkably subdued amid the disorder, but there is a limit.

I show her how to slide the coins off the table with one hand and catch them with the other, simultaneously arranging them in a neat pile on top of each other. "There you go – now what coin is next in value?"

"Eh?"

"I mean which coins are biggest after the tens?"

"Them," she says pointing to a two pence. I don't know whether the is putting me on or not, but I've come so far and I don't intend to spoil the record at this stage by blowing up, so I give her the benefit of the doubt and proceed with patience.

"No, I don't mean in size, I mean, after the ten, which piece of money will buy most?"

Before she can answer, Shirley says, in the aggressive manner, which is becoming standard for her, "Do you know what time it is?"

"Yes thank you," I reply sweetly. I am getting a bit irritated by her abrasive mood, but she is not deterred in the least by my slight sarcasm. Obviously it is a little too subtle to be effective.

"I *mean* – 'aven't you 'eard t'buses come?" she persists.

"With you lot in the room it would be hard to notice if a bomb dropped."

"Charmin'! Well it's quarter-past and if we don't gerrof we'll miss us buses."

"If you haven't finished your work it looks as if you'll be walking anyway. Have you finished?"

She smiles superciliously. "I finished ten minutes ago."

"Very clever! Christina?"

"Mrs Jacques says it'll take us a few weeks to finish," she tells me with a winning smile.

"So that lets you out. Carol?"

"Can I take mine home – I've a lot of pictures at home that I want to stick in."

"All right – none of you are short of an answer are you?" I noddingly run my eye over the rest of the company to check that nobody has slipped the dragnet. All accounted for. "Right you are then BUT – before anyone sets foot outside that door – I want EVERY table clear – what's yours out of sight, what you got from me, back here on my table."

3:20 pm. Half a minute of frenzied action follows like a speeded-up film, as their table tops empty magically and mine assumes the appearance of a scrap-yard. They surge thankfully through the door, most of them calling out sincere adieus to me. That is one great thing about them – whatever has gone before, they nearly always take their leave with no hard feelings.

I set about the task of reducing the debris from my desk and putting everything in its place. Bob Robins will be on his own with the buses so I go down to lend a hand. The fresh air will be very welcome too.

Surprisingly, when I arrive, there is no sign of him. This is strange for, although it is too early for the masses, either Bob or the people who hang the numbers on the buses for him, are usually around at this time.

Feeling a bit like a member of the crew who found the Mary Celeste, I stand, pondering the next move. At our school though, action is never hard to find and sure enough, from the direction of the farthest of the parked vehicles comes the sound of commotion. The voices that attracted me in the first place are rising to shouting pitch, to the accompaniment of a stream of obscenities.

When I arrive on the scene, Bob seems to be making a gallant attempt to keep himself between Charles Delaney and Susan Jankowicz who are the ones tearing into each other verbally. Charles often helps Bob with the bus duty, when he is not in disgrace, but what Susan is doing there I have no idea.

It's fortunate that the battle is merely vocal at this stage because Susan weighs at least twelve stone and is a fearsome proposition when provoked. Charles on the other hand is like a young version of Albert Steptoe – weedy. However, what he gives away to Susan in size, he makes up for in what may be termed 'violence of the tongue'. He can sting like a bee with his insults, whereas Susan simply goes berserk.

Bob is obviously beginning to feel the pace as Susan struggles to get at Charles. I move in and grab one of her arms – which is like catching a boa constrictor, so muscular and powerful – more like a man's. Bob and I must have a combined weight approaching thirty stone, but we are being thrown about like a couple of corks on a rough sea! Far from subduing her, the restriction only makes her worse, and the trouble is that I don't even know what the argument is about!

However, I don't have to wait long to find out. As soon as he is sure that Susan is under adequate control, Charles resumes his taunts. "Yer big fat cow! Yer a prozzy – that's what *you* are."

"I'll fuckin' kill 'im! She really is in a frenzy now.

"I saw yer – you an' Warren Dransfield, yer mucky cow!"

"I'll break 'is fuckin' back!"

"When Mr Fellows weren't lookin' – I saw yer – lerrin' 'im grope yer, yer prozzy!"

"You lyin' little bastard!"

"Prozzy! Prozzy!"

By now I am beginning to feel what it must be like to take down a big marquee in a gale as words fail Susan and she struggles with renewed ferocity to tear her arms free. Strong though she is, it is her grossness that soon causes her to run out of steam and she is soon forced to slacken her efforts.

This gives me chance to have a few words with Bob between pauses to draw breath. "How did this—all start Bob—?"

"Search me—I was out here with Charles doing—the numbers when—Susan appeared on the—scene—and they just went—hell for leather at one—another."

After pausing to listen to our dialogue, Charles renews his character assassination of Susan. "She lets all t'lads feel 'er, an' that in't all—" he hints darkly. "I wouldn't touch 'er wi' a clothes-prop."

"You wouldn't get fuckin' chance, yer short-arsed little cunt!" She begins to flex those mighty arms again, but I am not having any more of this. I tell Charles, "If you don't get inside out of the way at once, we shall let her go and what's left of you won't be worth burying."

"*I'm* helping Mr Robins with the bus numbers," he replies haughtily.

"*You're* relieved of your duties as of right now," I tell him. He stands there defiantly, hands on hips, motionless. "Righto, Mr Robins, we'll let her go shall we?" But there is no need to carry out the threat as Charles is hurtling towards the safety of the Barracks. "Now young lady – where should you be?"

"Mrs Jacques said I could come down and help Mr Robins."

"You don't normally help Mr Robins do you?"

"No but Mrs Jacques said I could."

"I expect you saw Charley-boy out of the window and decided you'd come down and sort him out more likely."

Perhaps the mention of Charles wasn't such a bright idea as she starts to contest the light restraint we have placed on her since his sudden departure. "I'm goin' inside to kick 'im in!"

What follows is like a Punch and Judy show – pulling and tugging, punctuated by, "OH NO you're not!" and "OH YES I am!"

This carries on until a quiet voice enquires, "Now, Susan love – what's the matter?" The Boss has strolled up unnoticed and from the look on her face is much amused by the show.

Immediately Susan is transformed. She gently removes her arms and affects the angelic look that she normally reserves for The Lord's Prayer in assembly, and says, "Nothing, Miss".

"Well would you like to come with me up to Mrs Jacques?"

"Oh yes, Miss." And off they go, hand in hand, Susan smirking self-righteously, the Head turning away from her to give us a wink of understanding.

"Ain't it bloody marvellous!" Bob says furiously as they disappear into the Manor.

"Yes – you know we reckon that Susan's dumb, but I'm sure she did that bit at the end just to make us look a right pair of prats."

3:45 pm. I stay and help out until the last coach vanishes down the drive, then upstairs to pick up my things and away. At least that is the intention, but halfway up the magnificent sweep of the Victorian staircase I am met by a very distraught cleaner.

Jenny 'does' half the upstairs section of the building, including my rooms. She is normally a very helpful young woman, rarely complains though goodness knows she often has good cause to, but now for some reason she is terribly upset. "Oh, Mr Bailey – thank goodness you've come! I thought you'd gone 'ome. Will you come up 'ere quick – I'm that scared." She turns and makes her way back up, glancing round nervously to make sure that I am following.

When we reach the top landing she puts a hand on my arm to stop me from going any further and points with the other hand, slightly trembling, along the corridor, "I 'eard this noise like moanin' comin' from t'passage – and you know what they say—"

I do indeed know what 'they' say. There is a tale that the Manor is haunted by the ghost of the last of the Whitaker family, the wealthy mill-owners whose home it once was. The story has received support down the years from many reputable sources, the latest being an educational representative who called on the school one day. He was very receptive to psychic phenomena, but his state of shock at what he apparently saw was clearly no sham.

Luckily the spirit is said to be benign and there is no evidence of any harm resulting from its odd appearances. Thank goodness there is no chance of seeing a cowled monk, which is my particular terror. I think I should die on the spot if I ever saw one. Still, the prospect of meeting anything from another world in this setting in the advancing gloom of an early winter's evening doesn't exactly fill me with joy.

There are three doors on the corridor in the direction indicated by Jenny – the art room, a tiny storeroom which is never opened, and the 'little room' at the end. "Have you had a look in these rooms at all?" I ask her.

She shudders. "No fear! I'm on me own over 'ere tonight and as soon as I 'eard that I were off."

"Right then, we'll look inside and see what we shall see," I say with an assurance which I certainly do not feel. The art room light is still on, and a search in there reveals nothing. A quick tug on the handle of the storeroom confirms that it is locked as usual.

I am beginning to feel much easier now, certain that what Jenny heard must have been the wind, which does tend to sigh around the corners of this old place. Suddenly, a sound causes us both to freeze. It is a low murmur, which could certainly be described as a moan. It is eerily distinct in the otherwise total silence of the corridor, and I can feel the hair beginning to rise on the back of my neck.

Resisting the impulse to turn and get out of the building fast, I move cautiously to the door of the 'little room' from where the sound appears to be coming. The door is ajar. I push it gently open so that at its fullest extent, I can see almost the whole room, and if there is anything of substance behind, it will have to reveal itself.

The heavy, old-fashioned door sweeps slowly inwards, creaking obligingly as in all situations of dire suspense and I let out a startled exclamation – "Ann!"

There, trance-like, surveying herself in the mirror stands Ann Sissons, gently crooning an unrecognisable tune. At the sound of my voice she turns sheepishly to face me. "Ann," I repeat with mingled relief and annoyance. "Have you been in here since you left the classroom to come to the toilet?"

"I've been gettin' meself washed an' ready to go 'ome." I suppose this is an affirmative.

"Do you know you've been in here *half an hour*?"

Her eyes widen and her mouth falls open – then she says, "Is that a long time?"

THURSDAY

14th November

9:30 am. I have just had to step between Delroy de Lancey and Stuart Parsons who are on the point of tearing one another apart, when I arrived downstairs to investigate the cause of a commotion which could be heard as far away as my office.

The reason for the ructions was, I gather, that Delroy was interfering with Stuart's beloved bike without permission. Stuart protested, Delroy resented, and the sparks began to fly.

When I arrived, Delroy told me that Stuart had called him a black bastard, which is his standard form of defence when faced with the possibility of disciplinary action. He has wriggled his way out of so much trouble with this ploy, that I now dismiss it without a second thought. I any case, as far as Stuart is concerned, I simply do not think that his vocabulary contains words like that. He has quite a command of foreign languages, speaking words like 'Paulo Rossi', 'Tour de France', and even 'Dynamo Tblisi', fluently and impeccably accented, but his English is strictly functional and I would very much doubt that it contains any obscenities.

A good talking-to seems to have done the trick and they stamp away in opposite directions. I don't want any trouble this morning as Thursday, barring accident, is normally a good day. I am free all morning to attempt to catch up on the admin backlog and in the afternoon we are due to visit Sykes's Pickles which is always a pleasant outing. Today will be especially sweet, as both Jeremy Knight and Andrew Miller will by now be 'enjoying' a salutary experience as a guest of Her Majesty.

9:40 am. So, with all this in mind, I lightly trip back up the stairs to do a quick inventory of personnel. Imagine my horror when I walk into the Leavers' room to find the pair of them leering jubilantly at me.

"Pleased to see us, Sir?" Jeremy enquires in sugary tones.

He is one of the few people who can make the word 'sir' sound like an insult. "No I am *not* pleased to see you. As you well know I do not like tea leaves. As far as I'm concerned, there's no place for people like you two with decent people such as we otherwise have in this class.

Jeremy characteristically shrugs his shoulders. "Me social worker said it weren't right for us to be locked up. Said it might do us some 'arm. Said we should be at 'ome with us families."

Bloody social workers! If I were to say my piece about social workers it could lead to me being locked up and 'done some 'arm'. But here we are with these two, proud as peacocks, thumbing their noses at the law, but worst of all, being seen by all the others to be doing it openly. Sounds like a good idea – why don't we all try it lads? Then there's Jeremy Knight talking about 'his' social worker in the way that Al Capone might have said, 'I wanna see my lawyer!'

"I don't suppose he mentioned anything about not doing it in the first place while he was spreading the words of wisdom did he?" I ask him bitterly. "I'll tell you something else," I go on, fuming, "as soon as we've finished here I'm going across to Miss Wood to see if we can't get something done about this."

I know that it is impossible, but I say it *pour encourager les autres* so to speak. If it discourages the others from believing that crime is easy, then the empty words will have served some purpose.

We are about to go our separate ways – boys to Bob, girls to Viv again, me to the Boss – when a hard rap on the door is followed by the purposeful entry of Little Albert with his head on one side. This is bad news! The appearance of Little Albert in our room at any time, means problems, but for him to have his head on one side as well, must mean calamity!

"Just look at this, Mr Bailey – it's riditlous!" he announces, producing with a flourish, a horrible green slimy milk bottle. "Do you know what this is?" he demands.

"Are you growing spinach in bottles, Mr Light?" I answer, trying to jolly him along a little.

He scowls in reply to my levity and otherwise ignoring it, continues, "I've 'ad to climb up and get it out of the cistern in the boys' toilets. They put 'em up there – goodness knows why – and I 'ave to clear up. I've another five like that downstairs. And that's only one toilet. I 'aven't 'ad time to look in the others yet. It's just riditlous," he repeats, lest we forget.

"I agree with you, Mr Light. It is quite ridiculous as you say, but we can't be sure it's these lads who are responsible. I mean, the toilets are used by all the senior school at lunch-time."

"Well – I don't know about that. Whoever it is, I 'aven't time to be muckin' about like this every morning," he insists.

"Righto, Mr Light, I'll tell you what we'll do. I'll get a volunteer to check them out every morning – how's that?"

He agrees reluctantly, though the only alternatives as far as I can see, are to carry on doing it himself or install closed-circuit TV, which seems a bit of an extravagance. Albert is all right, but every little thing that goes wrong in the school brings him flying to me with complaints. I have organised so many 'volunteer' groups to help him out with his various duties that it's a wonder he ever needs to get out of bed on a morning.

"Well, lads – anyone interested?" A selection of facial and vocal expressions of disgust promptly answer that one for me. It looks like an SFW (Send For Welsh) to me. 'Where there's a Squelch – Send For Welsh' is his motto.

"Right – on your way all of you, and Alvin – would you call in at Mrs Dolan's and ask her if I could see Ian Welsh right away please."

They depart and a couple of minutes later Ian Welsh creeps apprehensively through the door. I briefly explain the situation to him, stressing the possible catastrophe that could befall mankind if the right man for the job cannot be found. A gleam appears from behind his dingy glasses and he's hooked.

9:55 am. I set off grimly in the direction of the Boss's office. "Have you seen who's arrived today then?" I begin truculently when I get there.

As usual, she says nothing at first – merely sighs, puts a finger and a thumb to her bottom lip, sits back in her chair, looks straight at me and sighs again. She does so many things before she starts to speak that I always begin to feel uncomfortable. It's certainly a good way of taking the wind out of someone's sails.

At length she begins. "I've just heard on the phone about it – I presume you mean Andrew and Jeremy? I must admit I can hardly believe it myself."

"What bothers me is that every other kid in the school can see them laughing about it. No wonder the police are sick and tired of it. I don't suppose there's a thing we can do about it?"

She shakes her head again so I go on, "Well, if the powers-that-be won't do anything then I'm prepared to make a stand within the school."

"Like what?" she asks dubiously.

"Like this afternoon for a start. I'm not prepared to take them out of school and put other people at risk – particularly when they're doing us a favour."

She interrupts me for a moment. "Where is it that you're going today?"

"To Sykes's. They always make us welcome and I'm not prepared to jeopardise future visits by including these two. I don't want them walking off with their pockets stuffed with red cabbages and pickled gherkins." I tell her huffily.

"At least they wouldn't get far," she replies with a smile.

"About as far as the toe of my boot," I growl.

"Seriously though – I agree with you. I think that they should stay in school until we have a satisfactory solution. They can't just leave it in the air like this."

"Good. Thanks for backing me up on this one. I'll send them up to Gordon Fellows for the afternoon or see if Mr Light has any gruesome jobs for them."

"Oh, Ben – I almost forgot. You are free this morning aren't you? Roger Goldsmith rang in earlier to say he's been up all night with toothache so he's had to go to the dentist. He shouldn't be too long so can you look after his class till he gets in?"

"Oh f—for crying out loud!" I say in frustration. "I was going to do all sorts this morning."

"Sorry but everyone else is spoken for. I think it will do them good to have an hour or two with you. It will certainly do Roger good to be without *them* for a while."

"An hour or two!" I echo, horrified. "Still I'm not surprised he has toothache coping with that lot. I think I should have had terminal headache by now if I had them every day.

10:05 am. I dash back to the Manor to pick up my 'emergency kit'. This is what I use if I'm ever called on like this to take a 'one-off' class to cover for someone's absence. It consists of a series of pictures of people and scenes for them to describe or remember. I find it a lot of fun normally and a very good way of developing oral work, because most of them talk in shorthand anyway. Here at least they have the chance to develop their vocabulary, powers of observation, and the opportunity to speak uninterrupted for as long as they are able.

I need to dash, because if Roger's class are left for any length of time, one of the likeliest jobs is a 999 call!

I am greeted by a unanimous groan as I walk through the door. There is surprisingly little noise, no blood, only a minimal amount of rubbish scattered around the tables and floor – all in all, the signs are favourable.

"Right folks – gather round," I greet them. There is a screeching and scraping of chairs as they all come close. All that is, except Wayne Lawson who is still busily engaged on the unrecognisable model, which was occupying him on Monday. This is possibly a good reason why there was such a state of calm (relatively speaking) when I came in – Wayne was otherwise engaged. I can't make up my mind whether to insist that he joins the throng or to let sleeping dogs lie. I choose the latter course.

"Now – let's see what we have in here," I say in a Father Christmas voice, opening the emergency kit.

"Is it them pictures again?" asks one wretch scathingly.

I am deeply offended. For anyone to suggest that my lessons are stereotyped and predictable really is the limit. "No it is not *them* pictures as you put it. They are pictures – yes, but they are new pictures so there is no chance that you will have seen them before."

Another hand goes up – "Sir."

"Yes."

"Wayne Lawson's playing with his thing."

"Eh!?"

"Look – over there."

What he means is that Wayne is still working on his model, so I reply, "Yes I know, but he is very busy and working very quietly."

"Can I do mine then?"

"Can I?"

"Can I?"

Faced with this barrage, I have no alternative but to ask Wayne to come and join us.

"Aw, Fir, I've nearly finiffed. Can't I go on with it?"

"Sorry, Wayne. I know you're working very hard, but if I let you carry on, everyone will want to do the same thing."

He slams down the part he was holding, fixes the ones who called out to me with a murderous stare and, with very bad grace, joins the rest of the group. It's uncanny how, though apparently totally preoccupied with his model, he still manages to single out those responsible for his being called to heel. I sense trouble ahead.

He drags a chair from under a table and kicks it into place. "It'f borin' if thif," he complains.

He folds his arms and stares fixedly at the top corner of the room, so I carry on, taking out the first pictures. It is all about the letter 'b'. To give them a clue, the letter is printed in blue, on a white square, at the top of the page. It is a park scene in spring, brimming with things like bluebells, boys playing with balls, babies in blue prams, benches, branches, bushes, blossom, birds, bees, boats, and bags of other things besides.

I tack the picture onto the wooden strut of the blackboard so that I can stand at the side and point things out without obstructing anyone's view.

"Now," I begin, pointing to the letter 'b', "can anyone tell me what sound this letter makes?"

Sharon, a girl who always operates mouth before brain is engaged, shoots up a hand.

"Yes, Sharon."

"T," she pronounces confidently, only to be crushed by the volume of jeers and insults.

“Now Sharon, I’m always telling you to think for a while before you jump in, and you’ve done it again” I chide her. I notice silly little Andrew Green going over the top with his derision. “All right Andrew Green. You seem to know all about it. What is it then?” I challenge him.

“D,” he says, glancing superciliously at Sharon. Again the howl of mockery wipes the look from his face quicker than a slap.

“There you are, clever clogs!” I am pleased to say. “What is it then – anybody?”

There are a few unlikely sounds in the general outcry, but the overwhelming majority comes down in favour of ‘b’.

“Good. I’m glad that nearly all of you recognise it,” I say encouragingly. “So how many things can you see in the picture that start with ‘b’?”

“Bird.”

“Good.”

“Boy.”

“Right.”

“Boats.”

“Yes.”

Boots.”

“Why, yes – those boys playing football are wearing boots. That’s good – I hadn’t noticed that.”

“Balls!”

I look sharply at the speaker, but it’s the professorial Peter Brown looking blandly at me from behind his spectacles so I know that no offence is intended. “Yes – there are a few balls bouncing around the park. Thank you, Peter.”

“Bum!”

I wondered how long it would be before Edwina joined in. She has a complex about that sort of thing. Most of her conversation seems to revolve around it.

I try to remain casual amid the sniggers. “I might have known you would come up with something like that. Can’t you think of anything else?”

“Well,” she asserts belligerently. “All them misters on them seats is sittin’ on their bums.”

“Maybe so,” I agree reluctantly, “but couldn’t you have put it in a different way?” I realise as I am talking to her that the subject is the same no matter how you put it, so I let the subject drop.

"Boobf!" calls out the lad himself, laughing uproariously. "All the women—"

"Yes all right – thank you very much, Wayne. I think we'll have a look at the next item." I am about to remove the erotic picture from the wall when I notice a hand still raised. It has been in this position for some time but I have ignored it, expecting it to be withdrawn before long. The owner of the arm is Arnold. I only know him as Arnold. I doubt whether anyone in the school, apart from Roger and perhaps the Secretary, knows his surname, but mention the name Arnold and everyone knows who you are talking about. He is a shrivelled, pathetic little lad who attends sporadically and needs only the slightest discouragement or setback and he is absent for another month, so I must be wary of that pitfall. In other words, I must heed the unwavering hand.

"Yes, Arnold old pal," I greet him with great enthusiasm to make him feel at home. "What have you got to tell us then?"

"Rabbits," he informs me in a small but decisive voice.

"Rabbits," I repeat at a bit of a loss, playing for time until the relevance of his comment becomes apparent. "Now, Arnold – what about these rabbits then?"

"In the pictures," he explains. "Rabbits in the pictures."

I had forgotten that he is devoted to animals. I don't think that he has a great deal of time for humans, so all his affections are lavished on furry creatures. I can imagine him leading a hermit's life when he leaves school, living in a cave surrounded by his tiny friends.

I must admit that nowhere in the picture can I see the slightest sign of a rabbit but I must be careful not to put him off. "I'm sure you must be right, Arnold," I agree wholeheartedly, "probably hiding in the bushes."

"Down their holes."

"Yes, most likely."

I was hoping that this conversation might throw a smoke-screen over the question of the letter 'b', but the vultures are gathering and, before we can exchange another word, there comes a deluge of protest that there are no rabbits, no letter 'b', Arnold is a cheat, he's thick (that's a good one) and so on. Arnold withdraws immediately into his shell, eyes reddening, and I know that we have lost him for another spell. Sometimes you just can't win.

I take the picture from the board and replace it with the photo of a man taking a hunting rifle out of the rear of his estate car. The picture is straightforward and innocent enough, but I find myself anxiously scanning it for lewd connotations before I dare pin it up.

Reasonably satisfied, I go and stand behind the group. They all turn round. "No – look at the picture. I'm going to leave it there for a few minutes. I want you to look at it very carefully then I'm going to take it down and ask you some questions about it.

They sit staring vacantly at the scene. It certainly is peaceful so I decide to leave things as they are until they start to shuffle. Sure enough, after a while, one of them shifts uneasily, causing an epidemic, so I walk to the front and take the picture away.

"Have you all had a good look?" They nod eagerly. "Right then, what time of the year is it?"

Peter Brown throws his arm in the air. "Winter."

"Winter?" I repeat doubtfully, remembering the leaf-covered trees in the photograph. "Why do you think it's winter?"

He looks out of the window and says, "'Cos it's cold and rainy."

"No, you dipstick! I mean what time of year is it in the picture?"

He lapses into silence, looking moodily at the floor. Let somebody else be the fall guy. Another hand is raised.

"Warm time, Sir." This is Trevor Tyler, a willing if non-too-bright lad.

"Why do you think that, Trevor?"

"'Cos 'e 'asn't gorra coat on."

"That could be a reason, but sometimes, even in winter, we don't *need* to wear a coat. No – there's something that tells us *for sure* that it's summer. Let me give you a clue – think about the trees."

"What treef?" says Wayne rudely.

"There are trees in the picture," I answer icily and he promptly gives in, resuming his vigil on whatever lies in the top corner of the room.

Another arm is raised. At last someone has got the message. It is Zoe Briggs, a very plain little girl despite the almost star-quality name.

"Yes, Zoe."

"What time is it, Sir?"

"Oh come on, love – is that important?"

"We watch telly at half-past ten."

There is a general surge of agreement with Zoe. Her memory has rescued them from having to exercise their brains too drastically, and she instantly assumes the status of one who has scored the winning goal for England in the World Cup final.

10:25 am. Reluctantly I bow to the pressure from the class. They manage to persuade me that vital educational ground will be lost if we fail to see the next gripping episode in the series.

The television set is in the project area outside the classroom.

They each grab a chair and fight their way out of the door to make sure of the best places. Suddenly there is a howl of pain, and Sharon falls to her knees clutching her stomach. I dash forward to see what the trouble is.

She opens and closes her mouth like a stranded fish before the words will come. "Wayne—Lawson—'e—'it—me—with 'is chair," she gasps.

Wayne affects complete innocence of the offence, putting down his chair and spreading out his arms as though making a plea for absolution. "Fe juf' got in front of me and I walked into 'er."

Funny thing though – Sharon was the first to tell the tale that Wayne was occupied with his model when he should have been with the rest of the group—

10:30 am. The television programme is a big disappointment to me. It is about a rather anti-social mouse with a very poor track-record in house purchase. The theme song, sung with great gusto by the class, must be a regular part of the show, as they know the words by heart. However, I feel that the whole affair is way below even their limited standards.

Just before the end of the programme, there is a brief scuffle, followed by a sharp cry of distress. The project area is blacked-out so by the time the curtains are opened, the crime has already been committed. Peter Brown – coincidentally the second person to point the finger at Wayne – is sitting whimpering, holding his hands to his face, a trickle of blood coming from his mouth. My first concern, after ensuring that Peter will survive the experience, is to look for anyone not showing concern at his plight. Oddly enough, only Wayne appears to be totally in the grip of the next programme on the channel – an archaeological discovery in Tuscany! The KGB would be proud of him! I honestly do not condone gratuitous violence, but on the other hand, I cannot stand tell-tales.

10:45 am. I make sure that my charges are first into the playground at break, then pop into the staff room for a coffee. Rita Dale quickly corners me. She is taking one of the middle school classes after break. It contains a nucleus of hard-cases who regularly cause her problems and she would be most grateful if, seeing as I'm free this morning, she could send any sinners to me for correction.

In principle, I don't mind. Boys' discipline is part of my brief, but I feel that by taking this line of action, Rita is only adding to her troubles. She takes art throughout the school, achieving remarkable results with the material at her disposal. However, her lack of self-confidence is exasperating. I have often tried to talk her into believing in herself, but she persists in taking the line of least resistance, relying on me to bale her out of every trivial disciplinary difficulty. I am sure that if she would only once grasp the nettle, she would make her life ten times easier.

In the present situation of course, these considerations are academic as I have to tell her, "Sorry, love, but I'm taking Roger's class this morning because he's out having a tooth seen to."

She gives me a look of mixed accusation and bewilderment. "He's over there in the corner having a cup of tea. I've just been talking to him," she says as if she suspects that I'm pulling her leg.

I look across and there is the man, pretending to shrink out of sight at the mention of his name.

"How long have you been in?" I ask him.

"Just before break, but I didn't want to come along right away and spoil your fun so I thought I'd have an early cuppa and pull myself together before diving into the fray. Thanks for looking after them anyway."

"Don't mention it. I won't say 'any time' though." I go on to give him a résumé of the morning, particularly Wayne's part, and the possibility that only two-thirds of the planned vendetta has so far been carried out.

11:00 am. At last I am able to settle down to the elusive task of bringing my class records up to date. When I spread them out on the desk I am appalled at how far behind I have slipped. I have no idea how long it will take to clear the backlog, so I force myself to sit down and gradually chip away until the work is completed. It does require a great effort on my part because I have a tendency to abandon it and do something more practical instead.

11:30 am. I am feeling very pleased with myself at the unaccustomed progress I am making with the paperwork, when there comes a strange knocking – more like a battering – on my office door. I open it and there stand two boys, one of whom is holding out a folded piece of paper. I guess that the attack on the door was a combined effort. Judging by the look on their faces, I further guess that the paper does not contain good news for them.

Without a word, I take it from them and open it. It reads:

> Mr Bailey
>
> These two boys have been extremely naughty. Will you *please* punish them as severely as you can. You gave them a final warning last week.
>
> Thank you.
>
> R. Dale.

I study the note long enough for them to start to wriggle uncomfortably, deciding to lead them up the garden path before jumping on them.

"Now boys," I begin, all friendly. "You're with Miss Dale today are you?"

"Yes, Sir."

"Do you know what's in this note Miss Dale has sent me?"

"No, Sir."

"Do you know why you have been sent to me with this note?"

"No, Sir."

"No, Sir?" I repeat. "No, Sir? It's amazing isn't it. Every day I have boys and girls sent to me by teachers and none of them have *any* idea why. Isn't that amazing?"

They titter nervously, not quite sure of which side I'm on yet.

"We must have a rotten lot of teachers at this school," I ramble on as they nod encouragingly, "always making trouble for poor kids who *never* do anything wrong. Don't you think they're a rotten lot?"

"Yes, Sir."

"No, Sir."

They are beginning to hedge their bets, scenting a possible betrayal so I press on. "You two were sent to me last week weren't you?"

They look at each other before replying cautiously, "Don't know, Sir."

"Don't know – don't lie! You know that Miss Dale sent you last week for being naughty and I – out of the goodness of my heart – let you off with a warning. I remember telling you that I would let you off a whipping last week in return for a promise that you would start to behave yourselves and if you didn't – then the next time it would be forty lashes."

"Forty!" they gasp in horror. It is doubtful whether either of them can count to forty but it sounds a lot.

"Well two," I correct myself, though it still doesn't seem to bring them much cheer. The truth is that I can't really remember these two in particular amid the dozens who are sent to me every week in spite of Rita's chiding reminder about last week, but this is standard procedure. I like to go as far as I can with warnings before I have to get physical. It has about a fifty per cent success rate so it works as fairly as anything can, I suppose.

All the same, as Rita is only two doors away, we might as well have a check, so I march them along to the art room, for the whole story. The scene there is quite remarkable. It looks like a Cherokee convention. A line of luridly-painted children faces the sink. Rita is scrubbing tenaciously at their faces with a wet cloth. As many again are back in their places, obviously fresh from their paint-stripping if the pinkness of their faces is anything to go by.

Rita looks up as we enter and treats the two innocents with me to a look of pure venom. She is obviously beginning to tire rapidly, so our arrival affords her a breather.

"I thought I would come along with these two to check the damage," I say, hoping that it might give her some encouragement.

She wipes sweat and loose hair back from her forehead with the back of one arm, making a dramatic gesture towards the remaining six braves in the line, with the other. "This is the matter!" she says breathlessly. "Just look at the state of them." She points to the boys with me. "Those little turds kept sneaking up behind people and when they turned around these two hit them in the face with a handful of brushes all with different coloured paint on them. You can see the results. I'm about fed up of them. I've told them that you're going to punish them then I shall see Miss Wood and tell her that I refuse to have them in here again."

"I don't blame you," I tell her, then turn to the culprits. "Go and wait outside my room," I order them in a voice trembling with emotion.

Actually, the trembling comes from the effort of suppressing laughter, which threatens to burst free at any moment. The sight of those kids standing there dejectedly in line, their faces all colours of the rainbow, and the mental picture of how they got like that, is almost too much for me.

I have to allow them to go ahead of me so that I can discipline myself to deal seriously with the matter. It also gives me chance to say a few words of consolation to Rita whose confidence is once more plumbing the depths. I reflect on what a shame it is as I look round this exciting and absorbing room, which is such a tribute to her talents.

I walk past the quaking pair and into my room. I take out of a drawer what used to be a wooden relay baton, but now serves as a useful 'weapon' in administering summary justice. At the sight of the baton, one of them starts howling like wolf, which sets the other one off. They sound like Jeanette MacDonald and Nelson Eddie doing the *Indian Love Song*.

"You shouldn't misbehave if you are not prepared to take your punishment should you?" I shout, having to raise my voice above their din.

"Owwooo—"

"You first."

"Ahooo—"

"Come on – I can't stand around here all day waiting for you two to break the sound barrier."

"Oohoohoo—"

In the end, I have to resort to sign language to carry out the ceremony, almost having to crank their unwilling bodies into the traditional position. I make it well and truly felt, hoping that if their renewed lamentations are heard throughout the building, as seems likely, then it might act as a deterrent to others for the time being.

12:00 noon. I send them packing into the playground. I am on second lunch duty today, so I have time to do a few jobs beforehand.

12:15 pm. I decide to have a stroll down to take a look at the state of the football pitch. Although it is always a mess at this time of the year, I have never seen it so bad. If any more rain falls, tomorrow's game will be in danger.

I return to the Mansion to find Mrs Dolan waiting for me with one of her boys, David Goodyear. David is an enormously fat lad who suffers terribly at the hands of the others in his class because of it. The united efforts of his classmates and his gigantic, carping, middle-aged, widowed mother have, over the years, reduced David to a neurotic jelly.

He stands there towering over Mary Dolan's tiny figure. She seems to me to be trying to persuade him to say or do something that obviously does not appeal to him. I guess as much from his nervous mannerism – one of many – as she murmurs to him. His arms are folded, his feet firmly planted, but the rest of him is twisting nervously from side to side. The tableau reminds me rather of Hylda Baker and Cynthia.

They both look up at the sound of my footsteps. "Ah, Mr Bailey," says Mary with some relief in her voice. "Go on, David – tell Mr Bailey about it."

He stops twisting and stands up, making a quarter-turn to his left so that he is looking towards me out of the corner of his eye. I say ‘towards’ because he never actually looks *at* anyone when he speaks to them. His eyes always slide away so that they are focussed about six inches from whoever he is talking or listening to.

“Come on, David – it can’t be as bad as all that can it?” I say jovially.

He does not share the mood. Instead, he purses his lips severely, flicks his eyes over me for a second then looks past me before beginning to speak.

“There’s this feller—” he begins then dries up.

“Go on, David – tell Mr Bailey what happens,” Mary urges him.

He tightens up his nerve and starts again. “This feller stands at our bus stop every Thursday and ’e’s always drunk and—” At this moment, an invisible speck of dust on one of his toes diverts his attention from the tale.

“Then what does he do?” prompts Mary. I don’t know why she does not tell me the story herself and save time, as she seems to know it better than David. It must be part of her plan to bolster his morale.

He tuts like an old woman, looks heavenwards and tries again.

“’E swears at us an’ calls me Fatso an’ ’e pushes me about.”

“You say us. Is someone else with you?” I ask him.

“Shirley Baker. We catch the same bus up ’ome. An’ ’e touches Shirley as well.”

“How does he touch her?” I ask alarmed, because Shirley is a big girl.

“Like that,” he says, giving me a gentle push on the shoulder.

“You’re sure that’s all?” He nods emphatically, much to my relief.

“You think you know him don’t you, David?” Mary continues to build up the jigsaw puzzle.

“Yes, Miss – I think they call him Chaplin an’ ’e used to come to this school.”

“Have you any idea how old this fellow is?” I ask, but he shakes his head so I say to them, “I’m pleased that you came to me about this. Leave it with me and I’ll get back to you. David – according to you he should be at the bus stop when you go home today – am I right?”

"Yes, Sir."

"Fine. Leave everything to me now."

I go off in search of Bob Robins who is the longest-serving member of staff. It sounds as if this Chaplin might be about the age where only Bob will remember him.

I find him enjoying a flask of soup in the staff room. "Sorry to interrupt your lunch Bob, but do you remember a lad called Chaplin who used to come to this school a few years back?"

His soup nearly goes down the wrong way as he chuckles, "You must mean Caplin – Tony Caplin. Yes I remember him all right – a proper crackpot! What on earth do you want with him?"

I explain to him about David and Shirley.

"It doesn't surprise me one bit," is his comment. "A few years ago he was in the local paper nearly every week – drunk and disorderly, assault – then he got sent down and I haven't heard anything of him till now."

"He's done time has he?" This could be a more difficult job than I imagined.

"Oh, yes. He's done a couple of stretches at least for that and some petty things besides."

I send a messenger for Clive Coburn from among the groups of malingerers who are always outside the staff room at breaks. He is down within two minutes and between us we arrange that Clive will handle the buses this afternoon while Bob and I go down in my car to look out for this character, seeing as Bob knows him and thinks that he can probably recognise him.

Bob has some lingering doubts about whether we might not be better calling in the police.

I feel otherwise at this stage. The sight of a police car might put him off on this occasion, but we can't expect them to turn up every week.

"All I intend to do is warn him that we have had complaints about him and unless it stops, then we shall go to the police. Seeing as he's an old boy and all that, I feel that we are at least giving him a fair chance to back off, is my explanation.

"Well – fair enough – but he's the type who's likely to go offside if you cross him," he warns me.

"All right then – if he gets physical, you're there as a witness and we can then feel perfectly justified in turning him in."

12:45 pm. Bob is still not convinced but we have to leave it at that as a runner arrives to tell me that they are all ready for second lunch. I hate dinner duty! The original concept was laudable and humanitarian but, rather like trade unions, it has become too often a case of the tail wagging the dog. Imagine the reply if a building-site foreman asked one of the labourers to stand by the cement mixer during his lunch break!

We have more fuss and palaver over who sits where and with whom, than there is at a general election, although I grudgingly have to admit that today's event is comparatively placid. There is only one noteworthy incident – namely when Wayne clatters Ruth Tinker over the head with a chair just as I am saying, "For what we are about to receive—" His timing as usual is little short of professional. It seems a great pity that the talents from which he could earn a fortune would be judged by any court to be illegal. For the life in me I can't understand why he and Ruth always sit at the same table – they can't stand the sight of each other. Ruth's reaction to the attack is to have hysterics but as I point out in an effort to calm her down, she should be thankful that he hit her on the head, otherwise it could have been dangerous!

1:30 pm. We are all ready for the trip to the pickle factory. David and Shirley have been alerted regarding Operation Bus Stop. I have read the riot act regarding behaviour, the good name of the school, and the safeguarding of future visits. Andrew Miller and Jeremy Knight have been allocated a disgusting job by Little Albert, so off we go!

It is only a short walk down the drive and across the main road, so we can take our time. Crossing the main road is always an ordeal as I stick doggedly to my principle of non-interference.

There's always one though! On this occasion, Walter drops his handkerchief in the middle of the carriageway, then loses his specs scrambling around for it in the breeze. I manage to grab his glasses with one hand and himself with the other, hauling them both to the central refuge as the traffic pours through the changing lights towards us.

He is still determined to recover the hanky, but I am equally adamant that he will have to write it off.

"But um – Sir – um – what if my nose – um – starts running, Sir?" he grumbles.

"You'll just have to run after it won't you?" I reply uncharitably as I watch the square of cotton snatched up into the air and deposited over a high fence.

We crowd into the tiny foyer outside the office and I knock on the window marked 'Enquiries'. It is answered by the attractive girl whom I remember from the previous year. I state our business and hear the call going out over the tannoy – "Will Mr Sykes please come to Reception – Mr Sykes to Reception please."

"Do you fancy 'er, Sir?" asks John Bott, on his favourite subject, guffawing, his round farmer's face beaming facetiously.

"Shut up!" I retort furiously but he grins back at me unabashed.

"Mr Sykes will only be a few minutes, Mr Bailey, if you would like to make yourselves comfortable," the Receptionist calls out.

I don't know how we are supposed to make ourselves comfortable with only two chairs and a coffee table. Perhaps it is the custom to play musical chairs whilst one waits.

As promised, Mr Sykes soon bursts through the door, radiating bonhomie.

"Ah here we are – splendid, splendid!" He is incongruously and self-consciously dressed in a white smock, which protects his impeccable suit, and a Pandit Nehru hat perched on top of his immaculately-groomed hair.

"Hey, hey, hey! 'E looks a reight pillock," roars Peter Howard at the sight.

"Shut up!" I hiss vehemently at him, at the same time digging him fiercely in the ribs with my elbow.

If Mr Sykes heard, he is too well-bred to comment on the impertinence. He bends inside the office and comes up with a box of hats identical to his own.

"Would you all place one of these on your heads – splendid!" he requests.

There is a shrill outburst from the girls – "We're not wearin' them – they'll spoil us 'air."

I rave at them "You will do as you are told or you will *all* go back to school."

After a period of hesitation during which they scrutinize my expression and find it unyielding, they unwillingly don the hats.

"That's the ticket – jolly good!" enthuses Mr Sykes as they shriek with laughter at one another, and especially at me. I am thankful there are no mirrors about.

"Now may I suggest that half of you walk ahead with me, the other half with Mr—ah—"

"Bailey," I inform him for the fourth year in a row.

"Of course – Mr Bailey – splendid! Then you can change places as I explain each stage of the process."

The first room through which we pass is where the onions are processed ready for pickling. The smell is so sharp that at first it is difficult to breathe and the eyes fill with tears.

"Ugh – it smells like cat-pee in 'ere," snorts Carol Crawford wrinkling up her nose.

"Shut up!" I snarl for the third and final time. "If anyone else makes any more comments they will go straight back to school and wait for me there."

The first group goes forward with Mr Sykes who explains the intricacies of the operation. The others stand with me, watching fascinated as the two young ladies peel the onions with incredible speed, dropping them one at a time down a chute that carries them to the next stage. It is rather comical to see row upon row of onions of various sizes shuffling along like little round soldiers. Individuals disappear when they reach a hole of the appropriate size, dropping into their respective barrels, as if they have been shot, until only the giants are left. This is the ingenious sizing process.

The women work without looking up, as they are all on piecework. Our groups swap over, although I am sure that everything is really self-explanatory.

We move into the next room, half of which is taken up by the bottling plant, half by the beetroot treatment. The beetroot is first boiled in an awesome odorous boiler before being cooled and sent to a small gang of women whose bright red rubber gloves contrast with their bare arms. They work swiftly, grim-faced, pushing the soft beetroot through a frame of parallel wires which cut it into slices, then stuffing the slices into jars.

"Ooh look – there's Janice!" comes a squeal from one of the

girls. I look up to see a young woman in the firm's overall talking to a crowd of girls clustering round her place in the onion-bottling line. She carries on working as she talks, trying to affect the diffidence towards the job, which is an essential part of the ordinary young working-person's make-up.

This is a real stroke of luck. It turns out that Janice is a former pupil of ours, though before my time. She is an instant hit, a real heroine, someone with whom my youngsters can identify. They realise that they could do this job and the whole visit takes on a new significance – though not for everyone of course.

We pass into a smaller room where only two older women work. It is restful in here after the rattle of machinery. This is where the 'special lines' are made up. Piccalilli and mixed pickles come in large barrels and the women bottle them by the simple method of pushing the bottle opening against a spring, which opens a valve to allow the mixture to gush in.

"Come on, love – you 'ave a go," one of them calls to Martin Sissons. I have misgivings about the choice, but he steps up readily enough with his customary bashful smirk.

"Nice and quiet in here after the other place," I say to the ladies.

"We just go nice and steady in 'ere, love—" she begins to explain when we are interrupted by a wail of anguish. Martin is standing almost up to his ankles in piccalilli. Anyone else would have had the wit to remove the jar, thus cutting off the flow when the jar was full, but not Martin. He just stands there aghast as the pickle laps around his feet.

One of the women manages to reach over and snatch the jar away and Martin squelches and skids to the comfort of the wall where he stands dabbing his eyes.

"Never mind, love – you'd soon get used to it if you worked here," she says soothingly as they all, now the alarm is over, fall around laughing at his discomfiture.

The operation is now almost complete. We follow the cavalcade of bottles and jars along the conveyor-belt as automation now virtually takes over. The bottles are labelled, packaged in units of half a dozen and stacked ready for the fork-lift truck to take them to the dispatch department.

We are mesmerised by this demonstration of efficiency, but Mr Sykes explains that the whole operation can be fouled if one jar alone were to fall over. The whole line would be diverted and, until the fault was spotted and rectified, any number of jars and their contents would be destroyed.

We come together finally to watch, open-mouthed, the skilful manoeuvres of the fork-lift driver. The boys I am sure would stay here forever, such is the magnetism of his performance.

Unfortunately we are disturbed by a series of horrific crashes. We all rush off in the direction of the noise and when Mr Sykes and I arrive at the rear, we are greeted by the sight of jars full of onions committing suicide by diving off the conveyor belt onto the concrete floor.

Nearby, Peter Howard and Big Arthur are grinning conspiratorially at one another. Of course it is impossible to recall whether the entire group was together as we watched the fork-lift. I am sure that Mr Sykes, being the gentleman that he is, will not connect our visit in any way with the unfortunate accident. Still, I must remember to have a word with those two young men!

The visit concludes with question time and thanks. I always prime them beforehand with a few questions so that it appears that they have been taking a keen interest and have understood what they have seen.

I am very pleased that for once they remember the right questions in the right order. Then comes Mr Sykes's own party-piece.

"How many people work here?" enquires John Bott.

Mr Sykes, happily restored to good spirits now that the glass disaster has been sorted out, replies, "About half of them – hergh, hergh – I say about half of them." His own laughter anticipates the ecstatic reception of his joke.

"Oh," comes the response.

"You said, how many people work here, and I said, about half of them. I think you must have missed that. What it meant was—"

Mr Sykes's attempt at clarification tails off and he gives me a plaintive look. I can only close my eyes and gently shake my head. I am truly sorry Mr Sykes. I'm sure that the joke must have devastated audiences for years, but today, predictably, it goes down like a lead balloon.

Still, the disappointment does not deter him from wishing us a warm farewell, hoping to see another party next year (hopefully with a sense of humour) and handing each one a jar of beetroot as we leave.

3:15 pm. “Can we go straight ’ome, Sir?” a voice calls out as we pass through the main gate of the factory.

“I suppose so,” I say, looking at my watch. “But straight home mind and watch the roads.” It seems a bit mean to march them all the way up to school so that they will be in time to come back down again.

I leave Shirley at the bus stop with David who is already there, and walk up the drive to collect my car and Bob. He sees me as I pass his room and comes out to join me. We go down the drive and I slip the car anonymously into a line of cars parked outside a small factory. From here we can see the bus stop clearly. David and Shirley stand close together, no doubt more than a little apprehensive. No one else is in sight.

Soon a man approaches but he looks older than I would have imagined. I look at Bob. He turns down his mouth and shakes his head. In any case, the man walks straight past.

3:30 pm. A much younger, stocky figure, with a hint of aggression in the way he walks, arrives at the stop. He flicks a cigarette end into the gutter and looks up and down the road.

“Is this him?” I ask, aware for the first time of a slight tremor of anxiety.

Bob peers intently at the figure. “Could be – I’m not sure. It looks as if it might be him. The build seems about right but they change so much you know and it’s a few years since I saw him.”

We wait tensely but the minutes pass and nothing happens.

“Oh, that looks like the bus,” I say unnecessarily as a large, red, double-decker draws up. The doors open and swallow up the young man. They close and it moves off leaving Shirley and David still standing on the pavement.

“Shouldn’t they have caught that one?” I wonder aloud. “You don’t think we missed him – I mean when I left them to come and pick you and the car up?”

Puzzled, Bob shakes his head.

"Hang on a minute," I say, "I'll go and have a word." I dash across to them. "Has he been?"

"No, we 'aven't seen 'im."

"That wasn't him who got on the bus then."

"No."

"Was that your bus?"

"Yes."

"Well why on earth didn't you catch it?"

"We thought we'd better wait in case you wanted to talk to us," says David.

"Now we shall have to wait half and hour for the next one and me mam'll be worried if I'm late," says Shirley in her usual aggressive tone. That's a great thing about our kids – they are always so grateful whenever you do anything to help them!

"So will mine," adds David with much satisfaction.

By now, Bob has joined us and heard the last few exchanges.

"Why don't you go now and drop them off on your way home if you don't need anything from school. I can walk back up there, the fresh air will do me good," he suggests.

What a splendid idea. What a good excuse for an early night. And they say that woodwork teachers are not very bright!

FRIDAY

15th November

9:20 am. In the words of the song, *This is our lovely day*—, it was at 7:30 am when I looked out and saw a dull, dry, crisp day – a fine day for The Match.

It appears less so now as I again hold Delroy de Lancey by the collar with one hand, and Stuart Parsons by the front of his shirt with the other. They are both breathing heavily and glaring at each other. It's all about that blasted bike again and the accusations have been flying around like shrapnel.

This is quite enough and I tell them forcefully, "Look – I am going to say this once so listen carefully – today is a match day and you are both members of the team. I will not tolerate fighting between teammates. As soon as I have finished talking I am going to step aside and it's all up to you then. If you want to fight, go ahead, but if you do, neither of you will play or even see the game. If you decide not to fight, then that is the end of the matter for good – understand? Now what's it to be?"

I back exaggeratedly out of the way with large strides and view the situation – not without trepidation I might add – because I don't know where I am going to find replacements of their quality at this stage. They continue to look dubiously at one another for a few seconds then comes the great reconciliation scene:

"Soz, Stu."

"Sorright, Del."

"It were my fault."

"No, it weren't – I shouldn'ta said what I did."

“No, I shouldn’ta touched your bike.”

“I shouldn’ta left it where I did.”

I am beginning to feel a bit anxious about whether they are going to come to blows again over who is really to blame, so I part them again, this time from their embrace, and shoo them away in different directions. The crowd, which as always, appeared by magic, begins to disperse. I notice Charles Delaney among them and call him over.

“You haven’t forgotten what day it is, Chas?”

“No, Sir,” he sings out cheerfully. Match days are the high spots in Charles’s diary. He has long since given up the battle for a place in the team. The plain truth is that he is totally without ability, but for ages he pleaded and argued with me to be included, mainly because most of his mates are in the side. I was equally determined that I was not going to give in just for the sake of peace and quiet.

Everyone suffered for a while, and I was not the most popular member of staff. Then I had what turned out to be a winning idea. I put it to him that I badly needed someone to look after match day organisation in general. That means sorting out the kit, hanging it up on individual pegs in the dressing room, setting out the corner flags, checking the team list, and clearing it all up again afterwards. As a bonus, I also allow him to act as linesman for the game, and to travel with us in the same capacity to all away games.

We were all in doubt as to how good a second choice it would prove, but no one need have worried. He took to it like a duck to water and now he is indispensable to me. He is almost painfully conscientious, spending much of the morning darting here and there, wearing a pious expression as if it were more of a life’s mission than a job. I half expect to see him with his hands together when they are not full of shirts, socks, or shorts. There is no doubt about it – when he is motivated like this, he is a gem. I could recommend him without a qualm to any prospective employer, in this frame of mind. It is such a pity that the negative side of his character shows through with so little provocation. Perhaps by the time he reaches the Leavers’ Group he will have matured that vital degree.

9:45 am. Full assembly. This is the one day of the week when the whole school meets for assembly. It is quite an impressive sight – the hall full to capacity, big ones on chairs at the back, little ones on benches at the front, wheelchair cases at the sides.

It is always a very noisy affair and tends to drag on somewhat when the junior classes parade their week's work for all to see, but it is the pinnacle of their achievements and the looks of mingled pride and embarrassment are quite touching.

10:15 am. It is the turn of my lads to clear the hall at the end of the show. This is some task when everyone pulls his weight, but I have to be on the alert for dodgers on the one hand and the clever ones who try to show off to the little ones, on the other. They do this by trying to do too much at once, like Luke Towers. I spot him trying to carry a bench by himself. I have told them dozens of times that benches are a two-man affair, one at each end both for safety and for comfort. Yet here he is trying to manipulate a great, solid, wooden bench with his skinny frame.

Angrily I call out to him, and what follows is pure slapstick – amusing if you are watching, painful if you are involved. I made the mistake of not positioning myself very thoughtfully when I attracted his attention. He turns towards the voice without putting the bench down, with the result that the portion of the bench behind him smacks one of the little ones behind the shoulders, knocking him to the floor where he lies screaming in pain and panic.

Alarmed, Luke spins round to view the damage. As he does so, the other half of the bench strikes Martin Sissons right in the abdomen, (as Brian Johnston would have it) and he sinks to his haunches, gargling in agony.

"Put that thing down you idiot!" I yell at Luke. "How many times have I told you not to handle benches like that?"

His reaction is typical. "IT WEREN'T MY FAULT. IT WERE YOUR FAULT FOR SHOUTIN' AT ME."

"I wouldn't have needed to shout at you if you had been doing as you were told."

I feel a bit sorry for him though. He is a willing lad who is never to be asked twice to give a helping hand. The trouble is that he enjoys showing off.

I detail Imtiaz to help Luke with the remaining benches whilst Mrs Gamble and I comfort the terrified minnow then reassure Martin that the last rites will not be necessary, though by now his ashen face suggests that he's afraid that he's *not* going to die.

10:30 am. Clear at last and we all make our way across to the Mansion.

I quickly map out a letter-form on the board. "You all know what this is?" I ask them. There are groans as they recognise the shape of a 'thank you' letter. I stick rigidly to this formality as soon as possible after every visit. Besides being common courtesy, it is excellent practise in writing a formal letter. They hate it nevertheless.

"Do we 'ave to do it?" moans Carol Crawford, looking disdainfully at the board.

"Yes we do – we always do – so let's not go into all that again. Besides," I add, remembering her comments of the previous afternoon, "you should be writing a separate letter of apology after showing us up as you did."

She opens her eyes and mouth wide side in disbelief and points a finger towards her chest, but I ignore her and turn to point at Luke Towers.

"If anyone gives you a pound and tells you to buy yourself something, what do you do?"

"SPEND IT," he bellows, looking round at his cronies for encouragement.

"I mean before that, dipstick! What is the first thing you would say?"

"TA."

"I should hope that you would say thank you at your age."

"'E DIN'T GIVE US A QUID THOUGH DID 'E," he observes cleverly.

"No, but we had a very interesting visit *and* you came away with a jar of pickle."

"WE SAID THANK YOU WHEN WE LEFT," he carries on complaining at full volume.

"WELL YOU'RE GOING TO SAY IT AGAIN," I reply in like manner. "AND WILL YOU STOP SHOUTING!"

Defeated but still grumbling, they at last apply themselves to the task. This is one thing that, by dint of constant repetition, they nearly all do reasonably well. Of course they all work at different speeds so that the first ones are out having their efforts inspected before some of the others have got past writing their own address.

No matter how good they are (or think they are) at it, they all make a rough draft in their jotters first before copying it onto the appropriate stationery. This method ensures that they don't send something that looks like a fireworks display.

I notice that Walter appears to be in a state of considerable agitation, waving an arm about and muttering. When he is like this it is no good trying to ignore him.

"What is it, Walter?"

"Um – Sir – um – I didn't get one."

"You didn't get one what?"

"Um – um – a jar of – um – pickles – um – Sir."

"You must have done. I saw Mr Sykes give one out to each person, with my own eyes."

"Um – no – um – Sir. He didn't give me one – um – Sir."

"You mean you weren't there when he gave the jars of pickle out?" I am beginning to wonder if Walter had anything to do with the bottle avalanche yesterday, but his final comment puts paid to the notion.

"Um – Sir – um – yes, but – um – Sir – um – I got a jar of beetroot um – Sir."

"Oh, Walter it's the same thing. I called it pickle but—" My words are snatched away by a tornado of laughter from the rest of the class.

Walter beams happily, cheered by the news. As they say, 'he don't say much, but what he do say don't make sense'. All the same, he has given my memory a nudge, and I turn to Peter Howard and Arthur Davies.

"By the way – talking of jars and bottles, I don't suppose either of you two had anything to do with the mishap yesterday when all those jars came to a sticky end."

Arthur lowers his head and glances sideways at his partner, whilst his grin spreads slowly until it reaches his ears. Being black, it is difficult to tell if he is blushing.

Peter launches into his Woody Woodpecker laugh and says, "I know no—o—thing," imitating his favourite character, Manuel from *Fawlty Towers*.

"No, and I don't suppose I am likely to find out short of pulling your toenails out with a pair of pliers, am I?"

He chuckles at what he considers to be a compliment. He and his large friend are both in a good mood. It's Friday, there's a football match, and they are both in the team – Arthur as captain. He is not a particularly good player, but his 'physical presence', to use the popular term, counts for a lot, although I have yet to see him use his advantage unfairly.

In the meantime, Imtiaz has arrived, smiling munificently, at my desk. He spreads his book proudly before me. I look it over briefly before sinking my head into my hands and uttering a meaningful sigh.

"You are not feeling good, Thir?" he enquires solicitously.

"Oh, I shall be all right in a moment thank you, Imtiaz. I suddenly felt a bit weary."

"Oh yeth, Thir. You should be going to bed early, Thir then you will be waken up in the morning," is his expert diagnosis. I wish it were that simple.

He has spoonered-up his latest offering as usual. This is his second year with me – we agreed to defer his entry to the outside world for a year as a special favour to his family – but the words still come jumbling out. He gets the general layout right, but the individual words all need unscrambling.

"Ith not good work?" he queries anxiously.

I am about to sigh again, but soften instead and smile at him.

"You try, Imtiaz – by God you try – I wish you could get your letters in the right order that's all."

Gloom replaces his normal good humour, but his natural enthusiasm returns in no time.

"I try thome more, Thir," he announces defiantly. "I go thit down and write again. Thith time will be good writing."

Yes I know! "Tell you what we'll do, Imtiaz," I say aloud, "I will write down what you have written in your book with the letters in the right order. Then you can copy it and bring it for me to look at. How's that?"

He registers deep joy at this suggestion. He never tires of this exercise, although it is important that he has a go himself before finally having to rely on me. It amazes me that his boundless optimism is rarely dented. "Oh yeth, Thir, thith ith very good. I do good writing thith way alwayth," he agrees.

10:45 am. I hurry across to check on the condition of the field. It is certainly no worse than yesterday and I had made up my mind then that saturated though it was, it was about playable at the time.

The thing to do now is contact the Welsh Wizard. He never hurries for anyone, being naturally superior, so I have to sit holding the telephone like a toffee apple for five minutes while he is found, and presumably saunters down to the office to speak to me.

"Griffiths speakin'. Who is this?"

He knows damned well who it is as I asked specially that he should be told. He just likes to make people feel insignificant.

"Ben Bailey from Lees Bank. I'm ringing about the game this afternoon. The field is very heavy but—"

"Yew *don't* want to call it off do yew?" His tone affects shock and is heavily overlaid with provocation.

"No – as I was about to say – the field is very heavy but I think it's playable if your lads don't mind getting their feet wet. The conditions do favour us as we're used to them, but it's only fair to give you the chance to pull out if you feel that it might make things too uneven."

I give myself a congratulatory hug as a silence descends on the other end of the phone. When they eventually come, the words sound as if they have been passed through a coffee-grinder. "My lads would be prepared to play in a mine-field so don't 'ew worry about that one."

His customary urbanity swiftly returns and he continues, "So we'll be there for a two o'clock kick-off, old chap."

I loathe being called 'old chap', 'old boy', 'lad', and that sort of thing. I am beginning to wonder if he has a dossier on me – he seems to be uncannily adept at putting his finger right on the spots that irritate me. Perhaps he just gets on everybody's nerves.

"Right then," he resumes with an air of finality, "as I said, we'll come ready changed. Sorry that I can't be there myself, got a heads' meeting at our place. Got a youngster coming with them – Edwards they call him – joined us in September – keen – lot to learn—" He goes on like a tele-printer as I hold the receiver away from my ear and pull faces at it. Youngster! Lot to learn! I'll bet the poor sod leads a dog's life with that insufferable windbag!

When no more sound seems to be forthcoming, I reconnect myself to the earpiece and say, "Thank you very much then. Looking forward to ars—to seeing your lads later in the day."

11:00 am. Time for maths. We are currently looking into the mysteries of the pay packet, or rather what is left of it when all the deductions have been made. I recall being told a story when I first began careers work in school, of a boy from a special school who obtained work in a wood yard. He was told that he would receive ten pounds per week for his labours, which suited him fine. There was no formal careers work in the school at that time, so he knew nothing of income tax, national insurance, and the like. When he was given his wage packet at the end of his first week's work, he tore it open eagerly to find that, instead of ten pounds, it contained a little over eight pounds. The slip of paper inside the packet meant nothing to him of course, and was angrily hurled out of sight. He was a big powerful lad who had constantly been in trouble at school because of his violent nature.

In this case, after counting the money a couple of times to make sure that he had made no mistake, he stormed into the office, called the wages clerk a robbing bastard, and punched him in the face – result – instant dismissal.

As far as I am concerned, this kind of thing will never happen again, if persistence is any criterion. I am trying to get them to understand the terms 'gross pay', 'net pay' and 'deductions', for starters.

They all know the terms by now, but have great difficulty in hanging them on the right pegs. They tend to guess rather than pause and try to work things out. I have been fortunate in obtaining a textbook, which sets out the whole procedure with admirable clarity. Normally I shun the use of textbooks with my pupils as they are inclined to contain too many words, and are consequently off-putting. I prefer to use my own methods, but I have to concede that I cannot match this one for simplicity.

"Turn to page twelve," I tell them. Most of them rustle swiftly through to where we last worked. One or two, like Maria and

Alvin, glance slyly at what their neighbours are doing before attempting to make a move of their own. I notice Walter making a great fuss, peeking at his own page, then sticking his beak into next door's book, like a penguin dipping into a bucket of fish.

"Gi'e up, Walter!" protests John Bott, smacking him firmly across the ear.

"What *is* the matter, Walter?" I demand irritably, keen to get on. We really don't have enough time together, the class and I, for this kind of basic work. Two full mornings is quite insufficient. I feel that it ought to be at least twice as much, but that would mean a massive reconstruction of the whole timetable and a good deal of unpopularity for yours truly. So, minor interruptions like Walter's tend to exasperate.

"Um – Sir – um – it's not on this page – um – Sir."

"What isn't on that page?"

"Um – what we were doing – um – last time – um – Sir."

"Of course it is – here – let me have a look."

I stamp over to his table and whip the book round to face me. "I'm not surprised you can't find it you muffin. You've got the wrong page!"

"Um – um – you said – um – page twelve – um – Sir," says Walter becoming increasingly agitated.

"I know I did but you have got page twenty-one. You have got the numbers in the wrong order again."

I get back to my own copy and try again. "I want you to read very carefully through this page then I'm going to write some questions on the board for you to do in your jotters."

We read the chapter aloud, stressing the words *gross*, *net*, and *deductions*, which I write in the top corner of the board. I then write a short statement, missing out the vital words, which they must insert:

> (1) When we get our wage packet it has in it our ____ pay. This is worked out by taking our ____ pay and making some ________ from it.

Very simple of course, and they are even allowed to consult the book if they need to, though most of them prefer to work it out for themselves.

The best readers read it aloud in instalments for the benefit of the remainder. Then some of the poorer ones have a turn, and I cement it by reading a third time, putting it together more comprehensibly as even the good ones hesitate over the longer words.

Their heads go down and they scribble madly away, or appear to do so, as if it were a time trial, quality no object. As usual, such as Maria, Alvin, Walter, are trying to sneak sidelong glances wherever anyone is careless enough to leave work unguarded, but they are soon spotted and told to do it by themselves.

After only seconds, Big Arthur, Peter, Christina, and Carol are at my side. They are all one hundred per cent right, so I give them another little poser on the board whilst the others catch up:

> (2) Read page twelve and page thirteen and write down how many kinds of *deductions* may be made from your pay.

This will ensure that they do read through the pages much more effectively than if I merely 'read them', as there are quite a few deductions listed on both pages.

By the time I have sat down again, the pack is beginning to catch up with the front-runners. A few have simply filled the gaps in the order in which I wrote the words on the board, fondly imagining that I would be that soft. Others have put them in reverse order, reasoning that I wrote them in the order I did, to fool them, and thinking that they would be equally crafty. Luke Towers put GROSS on every one, in the certainty that, not having a clue, he would get at least one right.

I inform him that his bet is void as you are not allowed to bet each way when there are only three runners. He gives me an incredulous look and a king-size, "EH?" but I ignore him.

In short, nobody has got the problem right apart from the first four. The stragglers are still chiselling morosely away with their pens.

It is time to draw the whole exercise together. What happens is that we now complete the puzzle orally, the pack makes the appropriate corrections, and the stragglers simply copy the bulk of it into their books in the faint hope that some of it might stick.

It is rather like a cross-country run where the leaders are able to have a good rest at intervals, the main pack briefly rests, whilst the stragglers never have a rest at all as, by the time they have slogged their way level with the leaders, it is time to set off again.

"All right, may I have your attention ladies and gentlemen please? We'll look through part one and see where we went wrong or otherwise. I will read as far as the blanks and then ask you – by name – for your answer. Please *don't* call out or it spoils it for everyone. Christina, Carol, Arthur, Peter, I shan't ask you because you got it all right so it's obvious that you know all about it.

"Aw, Sir – that in't fair," protests the big fellow.

"It is fair," I try to reason with him. "You *know* it so there's no point in asking you. If we have no takers then you can fill us in at the end – OK?"

He still looks disappointed but accepts it with a wry shrug.

"Now what's the first one – what is in your pay packet when you actually get it to take home – Stuart?"

"Money."

"Thank you, mastermind – I mean what kind of pay – gross or net?"

"Gross," he guesses wildly, predictably taking the wrong option.

"Well, you're nearly right. It was a brave attempt," I tell him with wasted sarcasm.

There is a clamour to right the wrong, but I allow no one to take the credit for such a simple one. Instead I ask generally and am greeted by a gale of, "NET".

"Very good! Now if the pay you take home is your *net* pay, what do we call it before anything has been taken off it – Walter?"

A long pause ensues as Walter turns his brain upside down. "Um – eighteen pounds – um – Sir."

"Eighteen pounds, Walter? Sorry, I'm not quite with you."

"Um – you – um – told us – um – before – um, Sir – we would get – um – eighteen pounds when we – um – started work – um, Sir."

"Oh yes, quite right, I'm glad you remembered that. I said you should get about eighteen pounds a week, but that's not quite the same thing as we're talking about here."

Walter looks perplexed and mutters something to himself about me needing to make up my mind, but I prefer to overlook it. In any case, if I were to explain it to him again in a way that he would fully understand, it would take all morning so I have to leave him in the twilight for the moment.

To my utter amazement, as I turn away from Walter, Maria's hand is in the air. It is not there half-heartedly or apologetically, but proudly and with total conviction.

"Yes, Maria," I say trying to keep the wonder out of my voice.

"What time is Spiderman on telly tonight?" she asks.

There is that noise of shattering glass and hundreds of falling tin cans in my head, which always accompanies such let-downs.

"I don't know what time chuffing Spiderman's on telly tonight—" I begin to retort furiously.

"Ooh, Sir you said that f—word again," accuses Shirley Baker, folding her arms, pursing her lips and nodding to the rest of her committee.

"I did *not* use that word," I correct her. "I said *chuffing*, which I agree is not very elegant, but there is a difference. And what was that about *again*? I've *never* used that word in front of you, so don't give me that."

You did – you said it the other day when the boys were out 'cos we told you about it."

As the rest of the committee nod vigorously in agreement, accompanied by buzzing noises, I attempt to defend myself again. "I vaguely remember something of the sort, but I didn't use it that time either, I know."

"Did!"

"I did *not* and that's the end of the matter. Now, as usual, we have been side-tracked by something unimportant and if we don't get on it will be lunch-time before we know where we are."

I fill in the missing words on part one and we have a brief discussion of all the possible deductions from a wage packet in part two before they copy the exercises onto a clean sheet of paper ready to clip into their files. Each of them has a loose-leaf file, which I hope gives them more of a sense of maturity than exercise books. I cajole the slow ones along, as time really is flying.

"Right – next job. I want you to go round the room and look at all the supermarket adverts and prices stuck on the walls. I want you to imagine that you are living on your own in a flat. You have ten pounds to spend on groceries for the week, no more. Take your jotter with you, decide what you want, write down the price, then sit down and work it all out. If you have spent more than your ten pounds, you will have to cross out what you can do without. If you have any left then you can work out how much more you can afford to buy without going over the top – understand?"

This is fun and there is a general buzz of interest as they start to arm themselves for the shopping expedition. Only one person is not caught up in the enthusiasm.

Big Arthur puts his hand up and I nod to him. "Sir, why can't we do proper maths?" he asks me.

I know just what he means. He struggles with his reading and writing, particularly spelling, but his mechanical arithmetic is excellent, well up to 'normal' standards, so of course he likes to do as much of it as he can. The difficulty is to explain to him that mechanical maths is only relevant where it can be applied to everyday situations, like this shopping venture.

"This *is* proper maths, Arthur," I try again. "You have to *add* sums of money together, then *subtract* if you have spent too much or if you have some left over. Do you see?"

He continues to look dubiously at me so I continue. "As soon as you have finished this list and shown that you can get it right, you can carry on with your maths card from the table."

He nods, slightly appeased, but not completely happy. The maths set-up revolves around the attempt to achieve basic competence in decimalisation and metrication. At the moment, I am having a blitz on money and wages as I have said, and for the current shopping spree, I have chosen a number of colourful adverts with illustrations of various products and their prices, from magazines and newspapers. In the corner of the room is the maths table, which contains all our apparatus. It also includes maths cards – individual tests in the four rules, graded according to their varying abilities. If they have completed the assignments for any particular session, even a non-maths session, they are welcome to go and put in a bit of extra work on their maths card. Arthur, needless to say, would be content to do this all the time.

"When you are satisfied that your list is in order, bring it out and you can check it on the calculator," I call out above the hum.

This is always a very popular exercise, as they all love using the calculator. Unfortunately, it can be a lengthy process as many of them lack the fingertip control necessary to work it. This means of course that what should be the recording of a figure 4, for instance, can often come out as 444, due to their inability to tap the number then withdraw the finger smartly. However, things are definitely improving in this direction.

"Don't all crowd round the same one," I call out annoyed. There are eight of these posters around the four walls, but three-quarters of the class are clamouring round the one nearest to my desk whilst the others are virtually being ignored.

One or two people have sat down for a progress check so I decide to look in on them. Surprisingly, Walter is one of them. I sit alongside him to watch him wrestle with the figures. I notice that the first item on his list is a record player priced at £27.99.

"Walter you are a bean-bag! How much did I say you had to spend?"

"Um – um – ten pounds, Sir."

"And how much is this record player?"

"Um two pounds – um – Sir."

There is general derision at the comment. At least they have a fair idea of the value of some goods.

"No, Walter. You haven't looked carefully to see where the decimal point or the dash is have you? And what's more, what did I say you were to spend the ten pounds on?"

"Um – food – um – Sir."

"Well what are you going to do with the record player – barbeque it on Sunday then have it cold with chips and beans on Monday?"

The response from the audience is phenomenal. I must admit, I thought it was rather good myself, but I never expected anything like this. Walter grins gamely under the pressure.

“I don’t know what I’m going to do with you, Walter – I really don’t. Scrub it out and start again, and for goodness sake *think* for a little while before you dive in next time.”

Big Arthur is looking up expectantly from his seat. I am anxious to push him along because I need to extend him constantly to make sure that he works to his full potential, for his own satisfaction as much as anything. He is certainly a lad who is not easily satisfied either.

Unfortunately, progress in this instance is not that simple. He shows me his list of purchases – a staggeringly long one. I can tell at a glance that it must be well over ten pounds.

“Have you checked it out?” I ask him.

“Yep.” He answers confidently.

“What’s the damage?”

“Five pounds ninety-eight.”

“I’ll read them out, you check them on the calculator.” There is no danger here, as he has very deft fingers, considering the enormous size of his hands, combined with a sound mechanical sense.

We rattle merrily along to the last item. He gives the calculator a last couple of taps, grins up at me and hands me the figures.

I look closely at them before handing them back. “How much do you make it then?” I ask him, seeing the figure of £59.80.

“He looks casually at the paper. “Five – er – yeah – five pounds ninety-eight.”

“Look again – more closely this time.”

He looks intently, then suddenly picks up the slip and pushes it almost up against his nose. He looks quizzically at me, then back to the paper, almost as if he suspects that I have doctored the figures.

“How much?” I ask again with an ‘I-told-you-so’ expression on my face.

He takes a deep breath, puffs out his cheeks and slowly lets the air out through the corner of his mouth. “Fifty-nine pounds eighty-eight pence,” he says ruefully.

“Well now – is it real maths, or is it real maths?”

He smiles sheepishly but makes no reply, just looks defeated.

"Don't worry too much about it," I tell him, "I know you can do it. It just shows how careful you have to be when you're dealing with money doesn't it?"

12:00 noon. The task is far from complete, but we have a healthy portion left over until next time and as I said, it is something that they will all look forward to.

I am starving. For the first time this week I really feel in the mood for lunch as I step jauntily across to the dining room, cheerily acknowledging the greetings from children passing me on their way to the playground. It is still a fine day, no need to search the heavens nervously for signs of rain. It is one of those days that will remain the same throughout.

I hang around the cloakroom until everyone has cleared out, before going along the corridor to the dining room. My nose tells me that we are having fish for lunch. It could be boiled or fried, with anything at all, the aroma is the same. It always smells like an epidemic of athlete's foot in an infantry barracks, but the taste is marvellous, so I quicken my step.

The timing is good today and I arrive with only half a dozen people between me and the serving hatch.

A look at the seven dwarfs' table informs me that the fare is fried fish, chips, mushy peas, and—parsley sauce. The parsley sauce seems an odd addition to a fried dish, but possibly it's there for binding purposes, ie to prevent the chips from being scattered around the floor.

The seven dwarfs look up simultaneously and espy me with unbridled joy. "Missa Baileee—wook—fishyships!" they cry gleefully, waving their knives and forks about, to substantiate the claim.

It is not the 'fishyships' that cause me concern. Anchored as they are by the cloying parsley sauce, they are safe enough. It is the mushy peas, hurtling through the air like meteorites, which are likely to inflict at least cosmetic damage if one is wearing anything the least bit decent.

"Oh yes – marvellous!" I agree, treating them to the customary gormless grin. "Be careful though boys or you'll make a mess if you throw your arms about like that."

The last remark must go down as one of the daftest of the year, and the look they give me suggests as much. They look as if they have just come out of the ring at Bertram Mills's Circus. Still, you have to say something.

I hurriedly take my leave of them and hunt for the quietest table at which to eat. Today, I blatantly intend to shirk my duty by not looking around to see which of our numerous wrongdoers are up to their tricks.

Alas, life is not so simple! Before the first half dozen chips have found their way into my digestive system, I am aware of a presence at my elbow. I ignore it as long as I can until it starts to bleat, then I am forced to look up and take notice. It is a tearful little boy, holding out a jug for my inspection.

"Well – what's wrong with it?" I ask, peering into the depths and seeing nothing amiss.

"Sir," he sobs, "somebody's been purrin' grass in us custard!"

Dozy little ha'porth! I explain to him that in fact what he has in his jug is parsley sauce and not grass-infested custard! What is more, I explain to him, it is very tasty and he should go away without delay and enjoy it.

He gives me a watery smile of gratitude and departs, regarding the contents of his jug through different eyes.

I keep my eyes down for the rest of the meal to avoid temptation, intent on making my escape at the earliest opportunity. As I am leaving the room though, I am unable to avoid Kermit's latest piece of nonsense.

He always sits at a table of younger children, where he can play the clown and be the centre of attention. On this occasion I could just about manage to miss him but for the fact that my attention is willed on him by the eager eyes of the children at the surrounding tables. Being a very greedy as well as a very silly lad, he has filled his plate almost to the brim with parsley sauce, and is on the point of raising it to his lips to drain it.

Having seen him, I can no longer pretend to ignore him. He is obviously thrilled by the convulsed reactions of the people on his own table, as he pauses for a breather. Unfortunately his positional sense is not too good, as he has his back to me, therefore he does not see me coming.

As the plate is about to touch his lips, I grab the scruff of his neck with one hand, press the plate firmly against his face with the palm of the other and hold it there until he starts to panic.

When I let go, his face looks as though he has been dipping for apples in a bucket of whitewash. The others are aching from laughing, but the sudden shock seems to have ruined the fun for him temporarily.

A pair of eyes swivel towards me. "Aw, Sir!" he splutters, bits of the mixture dropping onto his plate and down his front. By now, the rest of his features are beginning to emerge and his foolish grin is taking shape, when I bark ferociously at him, "Get on your feet and go and stand outside my room. As if I haven't enough to do without acting as nursemaid to nitwits like you!"

"But, Sir – I abn't pinished me puddin'," he protests.

"You'll just have to lick that lot off your nose-end then," I tell him unkindly. "And from now on you can sit with Arthur and Peter and *they'll* keep you in order don't you worry." The look on his face suggests that the idea *does* worry him.

12:30 pm. As he tramps off, dodging outstretched feet and a forest of pointing fingers, I go onto the field for a final inspection. It may be imagination, but it appears to be the tiniest bit firmer. It is a fine sight. Charles has obviously made a start, as the corner flags are stirring proudly in the light breeze. I fill my lungs then turn towards the changing rooms. The outer door is slightly ajar so I go through the gym and push open the inner-door leading into the changing rooms.

"Hey, what yer doin'—oh, sorry, Sir!" says Charles as he turns from his task to see who has come in. This is one of the bonuses in having Charles as my general games factotum. I can hand him the keys without a second's thought, and feel completely secure. He is an exceedingly weedy youth as I have said, but he possesses remarkable authority and there are very few pupils in the school who would question it. Hence, there is never any skylarking about in the changing rooms by people who have no business there.

I look appreciatively round the room. Being an ex-professional, the sight of neatly laid-out kit is a pleasure to me – green shirts on the top hook, black shorts on the bottom one, with green socks pinned between the two, and the contrasting orange of the goalkeeper's jersey at the end of the line.

"Smashing job that, Chas," I compliment him. "They look a picture, and I see you've already put the flags out."

He gives a little simper by way of acknowledgement and continues mincing around like a temple acolyte, adjusting things a millimetre here, a centimetre there. Satisfied, he asks:

"Can I have the pump, Sir – the balls need blowing up."

You can't get away from it – he doesn't miss a thing, but I'll keep trying.

"Have you remembered to see Mrs Jacques about the pop and biscuits?" I ask craftily.

"Oh, yes," he answers. "She wants to know what time you want them."

"Good lad. Tell her about three o'clock when you see her please." What a man! I give in now.

Content that everything is on schedule, I return to the Mansion to get changed at leisure for the game. Kermit is waiting docilely by the door. I glare at him, to which he responds by giving me a sweet smile. I don't intend any further punishment for this – leaving him there for a few sessions will keep him out of everyone's hair.

1:00 pm. A time-check convinces me that it doesn't take half an hour to get ready to referee a football match, so I have time for a scan through the paper.

Incredibly, Luke Towers is engrossed in it when I go into the Leavers' room to look for it. The few other people in the room are so absorbed in what they are doing that they do not even look up as I enter. It seems to be that sort of day (so far).

I don't want to appear impolite by demanding the paper outright, so I try a subtle approach which I am sure will prompt Luke into handing it over gladly.

I clear my throat and one or two look up with mild interest. "Er – I was just looking for the newspaper," I begin hesitantly.

"I'M READIN' IT," Luke informs me as if I was in the next room.

"Oh – I thought perhaps you might not mind if I had a quick look at it before the game starts."

"IT'S INTRESTIN' THIS. YOU CAN 'AVE IT LATER."

So much for sublety! Still – it was worth a try, even with him. It will have to be back to the usual approach now.

"Come on Luke. I haven't had time to look at it so far today and I probably shan't have again. You can look at it later – you'll have plenty of time."

"I BRING IT DON'T I?" he replies rudely.

"Yes and I pay for it," I snap, "so you can hand it over and don't be so insolent."

Grumbling, he gives it to me. When I come to look at it, I have to waste five minutes getting all the pages back in the right order – something that really irritates me. Most of them have such untidy minds.

1:15 pm. I am in the middle of changing into my games kit, ie clad only in a pair of underpants, when there is a knock on the door.

I hear Kermit's voice assuring whoever it is that I am definitely in and it will be quite all right to walk straight in. The door immediately opens and in walks Elsie Davison propelling a small boy who is wearing a guilty look, which is about as much as I am wearing at the moment.

Seeing me in this state she becomes totally flustered and retreats from the room, shepherding the boy in front of her, and apologising profusely at the same time.

I pop my head round the door, hiding the rest of me, and explain that I will be ready in two minutes – she probably wonders what for! She is still so shocked at the recollection to do much apart from nod. It doesn't bother me in the slightest being seen in this condition – I take the view, rightly or wrongly, that I have nothing to be particularly ashamed of. However, when a woman sees you like this, it is amazing how quickly you can be in the wrong and the tale is going round that you spend your lunch-times exposing yourself to little boys and lady members of staff.

I have to make an attempt on the world speed-changing record to complete my story before the uncensored version is on sale in the shops. I hate rushing and in the end finish up probably taking longer than usual as I put my shirt and one sock on inside out to start with.

Decent at last, I open the door, summoning the courage to ask Elsie and her charge into the room, and bestowing another murderous scowl on the self-appointed commissionaire.

"Right, Mrs Davison – what's he been up to this time?" I ask, realising, now that I am myself once more that she has with her Wyndham Walters who, belying his picturesque name, is a little rat-bag.

He is a regular visitor to my room, and if memory serves me correctly, is now beyond the point of no return.

"Oh, Mr Bailey," Elsie begins gravely, "he is a naughty boy, this one. Do you know, he climbed to the top of that big frame in the small yard—?"

"How many times have I told you *not* to climb that frame—" I interrupt hotly, keen to cut through the explanations as time is running short.

"I don't mind them *climbing* that frame – that's what it's there for," she corrects me rather frostily, and recovers the initiative, "but when he got to the top, and thought I wasn't looking," and here she lowers her voice to a barely audible level, "he *weed* on some little girls who were playing underneath."

"NO!" I say, choking, trying not to allow my emotions to get the better of me.

"I din't do it on purpose, Sir," he squeals, sensing impending doom by the look on my face. "I couldn't help it, Sir, honest," he pleads, wringing his hands.

"That's what he told me, Mr Bailey," says Elsie folding her arms and primly nodding her head, "and I might have believed him if I hadn't been watching him, but I saw him take it out and *point* it at them."

I am quite overcome! The boy now realising the hopelessness of his case, breaks down completely and howls the place down.

"Shut up!" I command him. "And stop that snivelling. You're just feeling sorry for yourself. It's Mrs Davison you should be feeling sorry for – having to look after a horrible, filthy little ruffian like you."

"Yes, Sir – I'm sorry, Sir – I'm sorry, Mrs Davison – I won't do it again," he babbles incoherently.

I cut him short. "If I had my way lad, you wouldn't be *able* to do it again. Now I'm *really* going to make you sorry. I have more important things to do than waste time on the likes of you."

I take my training shoe from the top of the cupboard, an act that provokes renewed pitiful demonstrations from him, and leather him swiftly and soundly.

The shock paradoxically quietens him and allows me to inform him, without having to raise my voice above his pleas, that if he is brought to me again before a very long time has passed, not only will he receive double the dose, but will also spend a whole week standing outside my door, like the drip who is already there, in his leisure time. Mrs Davison thanks me and removes him from sight.

1:30 pm. The playground is deserted so I make my way straight down to the changing room. Good old Charles has let the players in and the sounds of the usual pre-match giddiness greet me as I open the door.

"Can we go out and have a kick-around, Sir?" asks Delroy.

"I'll kick you around if you don't sit down and shut up," I growl at him. "If you go out now you'll be jiggered by the time the game starts. With all the cigarette smoke in your lungs you've a job to last the full game without extra time."

This produces the expected jeers, but they all know the routine and soon there is silence as I give them my 'little talk'.

In spite of what many of our rivals would like to think, I do not drill them, I do not try to regiment them, in fact I do very little formal coaching with them. When I first took charge of the team they were simply running wild, everybody chasing after the ball at the same time. Now we just obey a few simple rules of basic organisation, and if their skills are good enough on the day, we will come out on top. I ask no more than that.

1:50 pm. "They're 'ere, Sir!" shouts Charles who has been on look-out duty during our talk. I hand Big Arthur a ball, keep one for the opposition's warm-up, and one for the match. Charles has the linesmen's flags and follows the team out onto the field.

I greet the opposition as they clamber eagerly out of their minibus. They look a treat in what appears to be new kit – royal blue shirts, white shorts, blue socks, and numbers. *Numbers*!

We've started already with the one-upmanship I see. The teacher in charge is, as the Wizard said, new to me. He is a tall, thin, anxious-looking young man in a smart navy-blue tracksuit.

"Ben Bailey," I say holding out my hand.

"Mr Edwards," he replies, taking it as if it were covered in pond weed. I dislike people who introduce themselves as 'Mr'. "I don't know how we shall go on today," he continues. "We haven't had much football. We don't seem to have had the time to get down to any practice."

Haven't had the time! It's only the middle of November and we started at the beginning of September! These people who start making excuses before they've set foot on the pitch, amuse me. Haven't had time! In my experience, there's only one reason why kids aren't given time to practise a little now and again, and it isn't down to the kids!

"They *look* good anyway," I tell him. The comment is snide, but made under a cloak of encouragement, goes unnoticed as he is still preoccupied with portents of doom.

"I hope they won't be out of their depth," he rabbits on, "only one or two of them are at a pretty low ebb at the moment – crises of confidence, that sort of thing you know. I don't know if their self-concepts will be able to stand a heavy defeat. It could push them over the top."

"Oh, I know – I know just what you mean," I reply enigmatically. He sounds like the latest textbook. I'm not surprised that they are all so uptight if they have a neurotic twit like this cheeping away at them the whole time.

His team skips enthusiastically away onto the field nevertheless, carrying their *own ball*! The Wizard probably warned them that we might have coated ours with paraquat! Their teacher and I follow. I switch off as he continues morosely bending my ear.

"You will be careful not to let it become a complete humiliation won't you," he calls after me as I plough through the sludge to the centre-circle. "I'm just afraid that—"

"Don't worry, mate," I shout back over my shoulder, "the game's the important thing. Just ask your boss – he taught me that," I add tongue-in-cheek.

Peter Howard sprints up to me as I blow the whistle to summon the captains to the toss-up.

"They've got *numbers* on their shirts," he tells me indignantly.

"Which would you rather be – a good player without a number or a bad player with one?" I ask him, and as he frowningly puzzles that one out, I add, "Win this one and you'll have them as well."

Gleefully he scampers back with the news as I greet the captains. I remember theirs from the ill-fated cricket match in the summer. He is a very muscular, wide-shouldered, mature-looking lad. In fact, most of their team look quite handy. At the toss-up, he stares arrogantly at Arthur as he must have seen fighters do before championship bouts nowadays. Arthur, predictably, appears more amused than upset at the treatment.

2:15 pm. A little behind schedule we kick off. They immediately gain possession and move menacingly towards our goal. A thin, peevish looking youth gets the ball in a dangerous position but loses his footing and falls flat on his back. The ball skids off his foot to Stuart Parsons, our goalkeeper, who promptly boots it out of play and down the banking – the herbert!

"Shitty dump!" moans the thin youth, looking distastefully at the pitch and shaking the slime off his hands. I cheerfully disregard the criticism.

After a while we recover the ball and they have the throw-in. For some obscure reason their player throws it towards his own goal, where Freddie Morrison gratefully accepts it as it sticks in the mud. He burst through a couple of feeble attempts to stop him and hammers it into the roof of the net past the helpless, petrified goalkeeper. The following second he is buried under an avalanche of congratulations.

"You fuckin' spastic pillock!" I pirouette like Rudolph Nureyev in the mud to catch their captain administering this blasting to his cowed goalkeeper. From the look on the latter's face, his self-concept must be undergoing a severe jolt as a result.

"All right – leave it out. I'm not having that kind of language in a school match. In any case, the lad could hardly have seen it, never mind stopped it." I tell him, moving as quickly as I can towards the pair in case matters get worse.

“Yer what?” sneers the captain. “What yer talkin’ about?”

“Listen, mate,” I mutter to him, moving closer still, “any more lip from you and I’ll bury you under this lot so just watch it!”

He looks amazed but makes no further comment. Perhaps no one has ever corrected him so forcibly before – if so, then it’s a pity.

For the next five minutes they attack fiercely and an equaliser looks a distinct possibility. Then Delroy finds himself with the ball at his feet in the deepest part of the mire. One of our simple rules is that if we have the ball in this kind of spot, we do not run with it, we play it straight out into the drier areas. Delroy though has other ideas, being in his own eyes the star of the outfit, therefore exempt from the restraints placed on lesser players. He starts to run it but trips over and loses it close to, and right in front of, our goal.

“Pass it you whelk!” I mutter angrily to myself but it is too late. One of their players kicks it forward to a solitary figure in blue standing almost on our goal line. He stops it deftly, turns, and places it into the net, well wide of Stuart Parsons, amid scenes of blue and white ecstasy.

“Offside!” There is no doubt about it. The lad was standing not a shade, but yards offside.

“Oh NO!” comes a disbelieving shout from the tracksuited figure on the touchline. I ignore it at this stage but it would have made no difference anyway. One thing I firmly refuse to do when I am referee, and that is to tinker with the laws of the game. If we have a meeting to *adapt* them in certain instances to special school needs, that is a different matter and I will go along with the majority, otherwise *both* teams go by the book.

I have lads with sufficient skill to be able to continue to play football when they leave school and I would not want them moving into open-age football and being humiliated by doing things like jumping six feet in the air to take a throw-in or the goalkeeper running round the penalty area like a clockwork mouse, with the ball in his hands.

Yet I see this kind of thing happen repeatedly when we play away, and it does the lads no favours at all. Mostly it is down to lack of knowledge of the laws by the referee, or lack of the effort to learn them.

If the offside was a setback, what happens next is a disaster for our opponents. The resultant free-kick goes deep into their half. Peter Howard takes control and a long shot from him trickles through the dispirited goalkeeper's legs. The air is filled with howls of anguish from one side, and the echoing of a triumphant Woody Woodpecker call on the other.

The captain's face undergoes four colour changes, and his mouth twitches violently, but he somehow manages to keep it shut.

Worse is to follow, however. Straight from the kick-off we win the ball and drive towards their goal. Little Anton Barlow cleverly lofts it over a mass of their defenders to Freddie Morrison, almost on his own, a few yards from goal.

"Offside!" comes the united appeal from field and touchline. I must admit that I am about to blow the whistle until I realise how clever Anton has been. He must have spotted one of their players standing nearly on the goal line, no doubt comforting the distraught goalkeeper, but at the same time distracting him and playing all our team onside. The shout alerts them, but not in sufficient time to prevent Freddie from delightedly thumping home the third goal.

"'E must 'ave been offside!" raves the captain.

"The figures in the action are still in the same positions as when the ball went into the goal, so I have no difficulty in pointing out to him, "He can't be offside when there is another of your players beside the goalkeeper between him and the goal."

"Eh – which one?" he demands ominously.

"That one," I point to the slight form in blue who, at this moment, is trying vainly to look invisible.

"You little prick—" the captain begins, then claps a hand over his mouth. I am tempted to say something, but he seems to be learning if only slowly.

We score another easy goal minutes before half-time, again due to flabby defending on their part. This provokes more moans from the opposition, particularly from one big softy who has slouched around the middle of the field, yelping whenever anyone has got hear him.

"That ball's too heavy!" he grouses.

"How would you know – I haven't seen you kick it yet," I retort scathingly, but several other voices are raised by them in agreement with him, so I blow the whistle and sweep dramatically towards the touchline.

"It appears that so far, the pitch, the referee, and now the ball, are all making a major contribution to the result of the game, in our favour," I announce grandiloquently to the figure in the tracksuit. "I'm afraid I can't do anything about the pitch or the referee, but if we could use your ball we might be able to redress the balance to some degree."

"This is terrible – terrible!" he whitters absently as he rolls the ball to me. "I don't know what effect it will have on them."

The new ball does not seem to bring them any more luck than the former one, as if by way of retribution, Delroy makes it five, right on the whistle.

2:45 pm. Half-time. Ours is a jaunty, confident get-together. I finish all I need to say to my lads in sixty seconds flat, before turning my attentions to the wake that is taking place at the other side of the field.

After a couple of minutes, I whistle for the start of the second half, but before we can begin, I am joined in the centre of the field by the 'Man in Blue'. "If it gets too bad you can blow the whistle early?" he entreats. "They really are taking it badly. I can't imagine how things will be with them afterwards as it is."

"OK," I say shortly. I really have had enough of this guy. I should imagine that after the game his lads will soon forget the result and be perfectly content that they have had a game of football. If they are at all like my lads they would be more likely to be worried at the thought of the slating they would get from me, than indulging in personal traumas or tantrums.

Strangely enough, the start of the second half gives us a shock. I mentioned at half-time that Stuart had hardly seen the ball and would be in danger of suffering from frostbite if we didn't try to introduce him to it right from the kick-off. Obligingly, Arthur does just that, but without first checking that Stuart is in position to receive it. The latter is busy tick-tacking to Charles on the touchline for his gloves, which he forgot when, play resumed. The ball speeds past him and between the posts.

That gives the opposition some encouragement and they rally for a period, but soon a sixth and seventh goals are added as if to punish them for the temerity in entertaining such thoughts.

After the seventh, the captain announces that he is going in goal. This is common practice at this level of the game. A goalkeeper lets in a harvest of goals then the best player in the team decides that he is the only person remotely capable of stemming the tide. This is quite likely but it does mean that any lingering possibility of reversing the result immediately disappears. I refuse to allow my players to do it, but this lot seem to please themselves.

Their players have pretty well thrown in the towel by now, and having lost the influence of their captain upfield, they only show interest when the ball actually comes within reach. Otherwise they devote their energies to chattering in pairs or staying out of the mud.

A stray boot sends the ball onto a piece of dry ground and bounces towards the touchline to where one of their players who has been sulking for about ten minutes, makes a half-hearted effort to stop it. By the time he has it under control, it is clearly over the line and Charles celebrates by waving his flag for the first time since the opening minutes. I blow my whistle in support.

"That weren't over," the boy argues, turning to me. I point out that the linesman's flag is up.

Charles, still wearing his altar-boy expression, sanctimoniously informs the boy, "You shouldn't argue with the referee you know." He really can be holier-than-anybody in this mood.

"Fuck off!" retorts the lad, unsportingly refusing to share the mood.

I groan inwardly. Charles has been a marvel today, but now, it seems to me as if a cloud passes across the face of the moon (metaphorically speaking). I can almost see him throw back his head and howl, the coarse hair beginning to grow on his face and on the backs of his hands.

What *actually* happens is that Charles's inability to turn the other cheek or come up with a soft answer that turneth away wrath, rises once more to the surface. He takes a firm grip on the flag and advances menacingly on the blue-shirt.

"Fuck off yourself!" he snarls, brandishing the flag, "or I'll shove this fuckin' flag up your arse!"

The familiar, imaginary sound of shattering glass and crockery fills my ears as I dash to separate them, but there is no need, as their lad takes one look at the murder in Charles's eyes and bolts.

I gaze reproachfully at Charles, but it is not necessary to say a word. Hastily adjusting his halo, he gives me a sickly grin and murmurs, "Sorry, Sir!"

During the next few minutes, as I am contemplating a premature end to the massacre, four more goals whistle past the captain. He is beside himself with fury, leaping up and down on the goal line like a caged gorilla, uttering the direst threats to the rest of the team. For their part, they daren't come near enough to give him any support with the result that he finishes up by giving a fair imitation of the little boy with his finger in the dike.

By now, his best friend is the original goalkeeper, who has belatedly earned his captain's profoundest sympathy and admiration for having to play behind such a set of useless gits.

3:15 pm. I blow the final whistle. Our team's three cheers for the opponents sends the crows protesting from the tree-tops, whilst their reply seems to be performed as a duet.

I am joined again by the Laughing Cavalier. "I hoped you were going to cut it down to spare them a bit," he mumbles dolefully.

"I did," I say with wide-eyed innocence, "I didn't play any injury time." They will be halfway back home by the time he has worked that one out.

"I don't know what Mr Griffiths is going to say when we get back," he says, half to himself.

A chink of light begins to show. "Look, feller," I say, turning to look him squarely in the eye, "tell that silly Welsh prat from me, and I quote, 'Never mind, Boyo – better luck next time – it's only a game remember'."

"Don't you like him either?" he whispers, darting a timorous look around him as if he expects the Wizard to fly out of the bushes and pounce on him at any moment.

"I think he is a pompous, garrulous, overbearing, self-opinionated berk! Apart from that, I don't like him – no."

"I hate his guts!" he snaps, suddenly animated now that he has had some encouragement.

"Well then – stand up to him – he can't sack you."

"That's all right, but it's worse than that, you don't have to live with him."

"And neither do you – remember that – you don't *have* to."

They spurn the offer of pop and biscuits, making the excuse that they must not be late back for tea. They seem cheerful enough as I wave them goodbye.

I go up to the domestic science room to join my lads at the celebration of their biggest-ever win.

"Sir – did you say we could have numbers on us shirts if we won today?" asks Delroy.

"Numbers on your shirts?" I answer genially. "Sure you can have numbers on your shirts. You can have rings on your fingers and bells on your toes as well today – but watch your step on Monday."

They all laugh and throw their fists in the air. They would have laughed and cheered today if I had thrown a hand grenade in instead.

The Boss passes me as I go down to the buses. "I hear we won today, Ben. What was the score?"

"Eleven–one. A school record," I answer, trying to keep the smugness out of my voice.

"Eleven–one! Goodness me – I hope they aren't too upset," she says, pride slightly tinged with anxiety.

"Oh no, I don't think so," I reply, po-faced. "We should have scored a lot more but I don't think they're too upset.

She leans back and studies me for a moment. "There's more to this than meets the eye, I think," she says uncertainly. "Perhaps it's as well not to ask questions."

"Let's put it this way – maybe there was to start with, but I think it's all straightened out now," I answer without really giving anything away.

3:45 pm. I watch the little darlings disappear down the drive, waving madly, mouthing "See you on Monday".

It's amazing how affectionate you feel towards them all when it comes to the end of the week – did I say 'a week' – it feels more like a month!